CW00418921

Lot: A Bible Characters Adventure

Amazon First Edition 2023

Copyright by S.R. Buckel

Published by S.R. Buckel

BIBLIOGRAPHY

The Mythcorp Archives:
Iconocop
Mythicon
Philicity
Orphan of Mythcorp

Other novels
Ichabod
The Light of Lexi Montaigne
W.A.N.D.
Lotteryman
Being PC

Short Stories
Mr. Sprinkle
A Collection of Sprinkles
The Shooting of Amy Rose
Our Ancient Foe
Last King of the Vampires (a *W.A.N.D.* prequel)
The Mirrorman (a *W.A.N.D.* prequel)

Non-Fiction
The (Psycho) Path to Success
Take it to the Bank
Bogus: The New Terror
The Patriot Resolves

Chapter One

Since Chedorlaomer's victory over the Five Kings, Sodom had descended into a nightmare realm.

Lot now prayed for safety just heading out to work or to haggle in the market. Men were often assaulted or worse out there, and unless they were members of some corrupt guild, women walking or shopping alone were known to vanish—turning up later in the slave trade or else a brothel. Lot rarely let his daughters have friends over, even though they were of age, on the cusp of marriageable days. The only time he felt it was safe to let them out of the house was when Uncle Abram came to visit. Not even these Sodomites dared harass Abram; he was known far and wide as the Lord's minister, a Mighty Prince.

It was Abram who had summoned his own personal house soldiers and gone to fetch Lot from Chedorlaomer's captivity.

He knew the gossip behind his back: 'Good Abram delivers him from captivity, and Lot goes right back into the heart of Sodom.' Such sneers were expected. They did not really cut him deep. But the look on Abram's face when Lot had told him he insisted on remaining near the scene of his confinement . . .

It still haunted. Yet he knew his calling was here, in this city.

"Girls, I am off to Hadad's."

Two stunning women, still young enough that neither had yet known a man, came skipping out from a back room. "Oh, father, must you leave so early? We were preparing the morning repast for you."

"Yes, with eggs boiled and strips of pork fat," chirped Ammi, younger of the two. "Your favorite. But only if you have said your morning prayers," she added with a wagging finger, teasing him on a principle he often set for them.

He smiled and kissed the top of her dark curl-encumbered head. "Indeed. I do love some pork fat. But I must be off to work, for many are my fellows who walk in darkness, not knowing our God. They need to hear what the Lord has given me to know. And what He can do for them."

"But they never listen to a word you utter," Charity declared.

"Except to mock you," Ammi added. "Why do you keep trying to save such men when they are so wicked as to laugh at your efforts?"

Lot lowered his head a bit. With a sigh he replied, "If not me, then who shall the Lord send to them?"

His girls had no answer. No one did.

As soon as Lot stepped outside the door of his spacious mudbrick abode, that old chilling sense of uncertainty and danger struck him. Whether it was the roar of street vendors flogging their wares, or the corner fight between two men or two women or men and women, or the ceaseless cry of ravens and dogs haggling over filth in alleyways, you could not escape it in this city.

Tumult only grew as he approached Sodom's busy square.

One could hardly track one's own thoughts under this onslaught, and Lot did suffer so. He found himself struggling to focus his mind upon God. It was an exercise often framed in futility, yet the man strove on with it, sending his recollections back to happy days with Uncle Abram, learning under the great man's teachings. How different things were then.

"*Hebe*!" A heavy and hairy hand fell upon his shoulder, startling the man.

Lot spun around. Looked up into the pig face of shearer Nahab. "Morning. How is your son? Has his rash healed?"

"No," spat Nahab. His messy dark beard often caught spittle in it. "Just as red as ever, only now it oozes pus in places. Seems your larky prayers helped not one mite! What kind of God is it you worship anyhow?" the big man spat. A glob landed beside Lot's right foot.

"One with His own will and who works in His own time."

A dismissive snort followed this reply. Nahab shook his head and continued on with a sneering: "If your God answers not your prayers, why pray them then?"

Startling shouts erupted close by. Near *Dandy's and Buck's Clothes*. Always there were fights breaking out there, and they rarely had anything to do with clothing, as that business was merely a front for Sodom's flesh trade. A pair of uniformed fighters appeared.

Soldiers of Chedorlaomer stood or lounged at entrances to important buildings or wherever they deemed it likely to gain profit, throughout Sodom. As he weaved through masses of people, Lot observed two soldiers heading into what he knew was actually a brothel. He lowered his head and walked on, kicking up dust with worn sandals.

In the twelve months since last Elul, Lot had begun a ministry to convert those soldiers to the God of Abram. On more than one emboldened occasion, he even followed one into a harem. The things he had seen there. Not just women performing, but others, and younger.

Some soldiers had laughed him out—those who noticed his efforts to turn them aside from looking at such things, anyway.

Others had listened, and even forsook such places.

But always and anon did they turn back to those dens of iniquity, when their flesh missed certain indulgences as stirred by the enemy of all mankind.

Lot continued on, walking past other examples of sin at work.

The shearers and dyers he worked for owned a cramped yard and adobe structure on the outskirts, within a few hundred paces in fact of the very fields he once owned. A few Gileadeans stopped and stared up from their balm vendor. To his left a few paces on, Lot drew the wings of his mantle tight, for a foul breeze surely played havoc with it; but also did he draw this gray cloth up to conceal his face from Jules, an effeminate member of a dance troupe who had taken a special liking to Lot, and spared no opportunity to try and seduce him.

Picking up his pace, he at last made it to Evil-Hadad's building.

Before entering, he was forced to step aside for a caravan of dromedaries, burdened with loads of dyed wool and one carrying what Lot recognized as packages of salted chops.

On entering the stuffy adobe structure, darkness struck first, though this never seemed much contrasted with the almost constant overcast Sodom sky. Odors hit him next. A rankness, sharp of blood and rotten meat. Most shearers dealt only with sheep's wool.

Neat and clean and no smell. But Evil-Hadad was a man of vast hunger and greasy ambition. Rumors around the site even said the beast had sold his second wife to an assembly of Chaldeans.

God only knew what those heathen sorcerers did with their slave women.

In a filthy back room, past sweating shearers who looked dark as Arabians next to mounds of freshly shorn wool, Lot reached his area.

The 'dyeing room'. What a rotten name, and he did so hate calling it that when describing his day to his wife. Sometimes it felt as he were the one dying, not the one doing the dyeing.

"Bout time," grunted night laborer Nimrod on spotting Lot entering. The hairy man dropped a clump into a large urn about the size of a grape press. "These and six more bundles need flattening and blued. And there be an order for twelve stacks of ermine for Chedorlaomer's personal household guard."

Lot liked that Nimrod never called Chedorlaomer 'king'.

After scraping with a comb stray fibers from his hairy arms and legs, Nimrod dropped a hand on Lot's shoulder. Then he shuffled out to collect his wages and head home for sleep.

With a deep sigh Lot commenced work, spreading wool out evenly and turning to fetch the clay vessels of dye. He sang old family chants. *Enoch Walked With God. Hens in the High Hills. Adam Fell but God Raised Him Up. A Mighty Man was Nimrod*. His fellow worker Nimrod had thought that last tune was about himself, and asked Lot to teach it to him.

This was part of his daily ritual, talking with the God of his fathers, singing to the God of Adam. It helped turn his mind away from his failures and hard state.

Slowly did he drizzle sapphire dye into the urn, all around, singing *Enoch walked with God, and he was not, for the Lord did take that righteous man*. Once the urn was empty, he would begin folding. This was tedious work. One had to laboriously fold the wool until every jot and cravat were colored. Without proper gloves, it would stain your hands for long days afterward.

Looking around, Lot failed to spot his gloves. Normally they lay tucked in a wooden pigeonhole behind clay urns.

Not today.

Pursing his lips and blowing out, Lot groaned. "Ham." Had to be Ham. That fat oaf was forever making mischief, harassing Lot, physically shoving him around or otherwise making his life a pitted stay in Gehenna.

Upon an opportune moment Lot would try and fetch his kid gloves. The dye would dry and this batch be ruined if he now wandered off to find Ham and try and force the big man to return them.

Tromping back to the giant wool blend, Lot stuffed his hands in and began to fold.

Within moments they were stained a deep sky blue. They would remain that way until Irith could procure some unguent, maybe a skin of Ezra's Oil.

By afternoon mealtime Lot's shoulders burned and his arms ached, but he had finished his quota and emptied the vat to head over to a street vendor who did often call at this very hour, to sell victuals to Evil-Hadad's crew.

Outside at Elizabeth's cart, a dual tiered wood buggy pulled by a pair of dark gray and ornery donkeys, stood Ham. The porcine fellow was up to his old tricks. Jawing what he thought were cunning solicitations at poor frightened Liz, cracking up his lackeys, and helping himself to a little extra food. Always the beefy man paid for his meals, but always did he also help himself to free desserts.

Shaking his head and sighing, Lot asked the Lord *'Give me courage and words to face my enemy.'* And stepped down into a street of mud.

Surprising himself as well as Ham, on reaching the big oaf Lot grabbed his thick hairy wrist and made him drop the cake he was filching. "You need to stop stealing from Elizabeth. You heard her, she is getting in trouble with her father-in-law for those lost goods you take."

At first he thought Ham might strike him (as the man had done on two other occasions), but on seeing Lot's blue hands, he recoiled.

Then Ham belched a hearty laugh. His lackey's took up the refrain.

"Listen to little lord Lot here!" bellowed Ham in his rumbling voice. Half the street looked up at the commotion. "You need to stop stealing," mocking Lot's Urian accent.

Lot bent down and retrieved the cake, handing it to Elizabeth, a tiny woman whose pierced ears and nose and revealing garments contrasted her meekness. She skipped away from the scowling Ham. Prepared her cart to move on up the street.

On observing the renewed attention Ham was giving her, Lot decided to give her an opportunity to escape his wrath. "Ham, did you take my gloves?'

That worked.

Ham turned from his female prey to his male prey. Waddled his bulk over to Lot. Scowled down at him. "Take your gloves? Why?" Here he snatched Lot's hand, sneered at it and flung it aside. "Yours would not fit my hands, these man hands."

Embracing the strength his God seemed to be lending him, Lot raised his eyes to look up at his enemy. "Y-yet still you may have stolen them to sell them."

No one knew the strength it took for this small man to stand up daily to his large and intimidating enemies. And he had many enemies. A city full of them. Not even Irith knew. He kept the worst parts of his day from her, to spare her the brutality of Sodom's ugliness. Certainly he told nothing of his fears, his constant trembling just going out his door each day, to

15

his daughters. They lived sheltered lives, thinking what few rough things he did reveal of Sodom to be exaggerations.

Cocking his head like a bird of prey, Ham seemed to waiver between wanting to laugh at Lot or strangle him.

"That do sound like a wise idea. Maybe I did do that, at that. I do suppose you shall never know." And Ham shoulder-slammed Lot as he passed by.

A crowd had gathered by now, in addition to their cackling fellow workers. Like jackals they all seemed to Lot. Big eyes and jagged pointing fingers and yellow teeth.

Trembling but believing the Lord wanted him to stand up for righteousness, Lot said firmly "If you stole my gloves, you would prove yourself able to repent, by confessing and returning them."

His poignant words now did cause Ham to pause. Lot reflected that the man's back seemed a wall of flesh covered in cow hide.

Ham turned on him. Grabbed his tunic and hoisted Lot till the smaller man was on his toes, pulled face to face with his enemy. Ham snarled and spat. "Thought I when first you came to our city, that you were a pompous snubber. Right I was, eh? Think you can teach us your foreign customs and tell us what god to follow, just for because you are kin to Abram?" Drool and spittle fell onto Lot's face as he tried to escape. Ham's breath like dung. "Abram be a great man, and rich. You were once rich, ha, but lost it all now. And *never* great was Lot. Just another rum Hebrew."

"Fine," Lot managed, repulsed and disheartened. "Forget about the gloves. I will speak to you no longer except for work matters. Your spirit is lost. I shall not seek to retrieve it for you again. Judge ye this fair?"

Ham set him down, shoved him in the shoulder hard enough to set him reeling, and then snorted. "Little lord Lot begins to accept what he really is: a worm."

They trekked back into Evil-Hadad's building. Crowds dispersed, sighs expressing their disappointment at not getting a more violent show. But as Lot dusted himself, he smiled. Elizabeth had managed to escape—without losing any product.

It felt good to know he had managed to at least help out a woman today.

Even if his hands were stained blue and he now had to come up with another three silver coins to buy new gloves.

Upon resuming work—following a meager repast of hard unleavened cake and a few raisins—Lot strove to whistle hymns. His spirit was not in it. Yet so focused on his task at hand and on the striving to worship his God, Lot was surprised to find Evil-Hadad himself standing behind him. He nearly jumped at the sight. Most Sodomites had a dark olive skin tone, but Evil-Hadad was Ethiopian, and thus could blend into shadows when he chose—which he often did.

Lot set a bundle down and faced his employer.

"Your hands are blue," in a grunting accented voice.

"Yes, my gloves were stolen again—"

"Collect your wages. You are done here for two weeks. Heard I what ransomed fodder you pulled against Ham earlier. Trouble you westerners are, always trouble to me."

Having forgotten that Ham was Evil-Hadad's kin, Lot now realized his mistake in publicly confronting the man about his wicked habits. He would have argued. Might have tried to keep his labor unbroken with vows or even reduced wages. But everyone knew Ethiopians never back down from their word, and Evil-Hadad was no exception.

Shuffling out to the wage-bearer's small, guarded station, Lot collected his wages and left the adobe building.

Careful to avoid alleys and shady dens of iniquity (like Ashtoreth's Flesh Market), Lot quickened his pace, wondering how he might assure Irith they did possess money sufficient to see them through this latest tribulation.

That consideration would have to wait.

For at home, his wife had far more dire news for him.

Chapter Two

Pacing in her naked feet, Irith waited upon the stone porch outside their door.

On sight Lot knew something was wrong, for she was wringing her hands too. Hot breeze ruffled her plain double-layered linen tunic and sent her raven hair flailing. Lot had always loved Irith's long lochs. Often she did tease him that he married her for her hair, and the rest of her just came with it.

"Oh Lot, they have gone. I looked and looked and they are nowhere here. What shall we do?"

Swift as a swallow Lot darted into their house. Searched every room quick as thought (this did not take long, as it was not a large abode). Came back out to his worrying wife. "They took their bags but not their face paints. They must be planning to return." This was meant to comfort, but he understood why Irith did not appear comforted.

Youth on their own were not safe in the streets of Sodom, especially youths unfamiliar with Sodom's labyrinthine streets and Babylonian customs.

He hugged his wife. The bride trembled but after some time did calm a bit. When he released her, Lot placed his hands on her shoulders. Now, Irith was a petite woman, but Lot stood not much taller, and so he gazed straight into her eyes and assured her: "I will take Ebenezer and together search, and so we shall find them."

She nodded.

Only now as Lot drew his hands back did she observe their unashamed blueness. There was no need for him to explain. They had been through this before.

Irith sighed and made her husband promise he would return their girls to her before the following morn.

By the time he had gone to their neighbors and explained the situation, and received

Ebenezer's promise of aid, and given his own vow to Ebenezer's wife Sera that he would be safe, they set out with Seth lights. A creation of Ebenezer's, these were simple cheap rushlights cleverly amplified by a backing of highly polished bronze.

Thunder rumbled overhead in gathering dusk as they set out on foot.

On Sidon Street Ebenezer hacked and spoke up. A hunched and grizzled man with a voice like a rockslide, he was Lot's only trustworthy neighbor. "I trust you know where to look? Tis a big city, old boy. We mayhap end up like two men trying to thread a needle through a pile of hay."

Lot turned right down a filthy alley, a shortcut. "They have a friend who visits them on occasion. This girl gave them her address."

Ebenezer shuffled faster to keep up with Lot, avoiding slopping through gutter refuse. "Well, my friend, I do hope you know that address too. Elsewise

we must trust to the providence of your God. And
that be often much the same as casting . . . *lots*."

Despite his old friend's decent nature,
Ebenezer had never taken to the God of Abram,
whom Lot had explained to him more than once.

"By my *God's* grace, I overheard them not
three nights ago. I have the address. I know not
why she told them, for she knows we keep the
girls home safe." He coughed on acrid city air. "It is
in the Gog district." Though grateful and glad to be
able to share this and dispel his neighbor's doubt
while honoring the God of his uncle Abram, Lot
knew it would not come as comforting news. Gog
district was known for extreme degradation and
thievery. Even among the average Sodomite, the
Gog slums were normally avoided if possible.

Even soldiers of Chedorlaomer went not
there—save for personal sinful indulgences.

Following an appropriate term of silence,
Ebenezer cleared his throat and in a low murmur

said, "How did well-raised girls like your own meet a muddy anyway?"

Scanning for lurkers beneath second floor porches and behind stout mudbrick columns, Lot led the way along a stretch of dark alley. It reeked of rodent corpses and woven rugs soiled with urine. "She appeared at our door one day, this girl," Lot explained as they walked, always careful to keep his voice down. Both men sidled along the left to avoid a scuffle on the other side. "Irith took pity on her, for she did look an urchin, and we suspected she had been defiled. So Irith invited her in, and the girls bathed her, gave her clean garments and tried to explain our ways to her."

"And she converted, like that?" Ebenezer sounded suspicious—a common tone.

"Indeed. Took to our way of life a sliver too quickly, now I think on it. Was an angel of the Lord to my girls. Hmm. Soon enough—"

"They started heeding *her* words and stories."

For a time they trod on in sullen silence, the younger Lot creeping ahead apace.

At length Lot paused to consider their direction. Ebenezer came huffing up beside him, locked eyes with Lot. "You think she was a mole? One of the Rat King's set-up people?"

It was a horrific thought to contemplate. But there was little doubt at this point in Lot's mind. The hedonists trafficked in human flesh. Mostly it were boys and men, but there was some demand for young virgin girls. A chill traveled along his body. To shake it off, Lot patted Ebenezer on the shoulder and sped off toward Gog's district.

Night came on, darkness descending like a heavy canvas enclosure.

Besides their own Seth lights, illumination glowed but dull in decrepit abodes either side, most flickering weakly from second-story flats. You could see into some of them. See things Lot wished he did not see. Decided upon keeping his eyes looking straight ahead.

At last they reached a left turn onto a wide street paved in pitted mudbrick. It looked to be Leviathan's gaping maw.

"Sodom's own personal Sheol," Ebenezer hissed. "I am not so young that I fear to confess, I might water my tunic right here. I am terrified to enter this district."

"So am I," admitted Lot.

Yet he strode forward, not waiting for Ebenezer.

As his old friend cursed behind in lingering shame, a vast district opened before Lot, a decaying sight of old Uruk style towers interspersed with single-story harems, where any lust could be satisfied for as little as a few homers of sugar. Many more lights flickered here than in Sodom proper. Gog never slept. Under his own meager light, Lot knelt and prayed for guidance and protection.

The man then strode forward, all atremble.

Of structures he passed all were named with unlikely ennobled symbols, which most anyone could identify without being literate, for they were known throughout the east, carven symbols representing: *Gosher. Ahazen. Keniah. Magone. Lesser-Baal.* Each stood for the name of its businessman. Or as Lot thought of them: *Those men of ill-repute, men of sin.*

At a decrepit wooden water vat, reeking of sulfur, Lot passed a group. Two of them groped at each other; their motions seemed violent and as if the smaller were struggling, but as he trod by, Lot realized they were both of them moaning while the others made cat and dog noises in encouragement.

Finally, after what seemed ages of searching and wandering around in quest, he found a solitary figure. This one—seemingly a man at first sight, though a shroud hindered clarity—was rolling small painted stones across a rickety trestle table, beneath a misshapen rushlight. Lot asked where he might find Azrael's Cowry Shell. The figure slowly turned its head up to him. That hanging rushlight cast eerie luminescence over the face.

A snorted reply.

"Forgive me, I did not hear you?"

Slowly did the figure raise its face again. Lot thought he saw a vision of an unclean spirit wrapped in flies, and recoiled a step.

"Thar way, cross de square. Azrael sells de girls," this in a voice spread thin by wine. "Scum live there. Azrael's little imps, doing his evil bidding. You want a boy? Clean? I know place, you get one cheap."

Backing further away, Lot headed toward the square.

He still could not have said if that person were a man. Not for sure.

His own light burning low, Lot strode swiftly across this large flat section of Gog, avoiding refuse and dog waste and other things that attacked his nose. Dead rotting things, meat still on the bone. On the other side he came upon a sturdy building, gray and drab and foreboding, stretching three uneven stories high and nigh on half a city block wide.

"Lord, be my refuge, and lead me to my girls."

Distant hum of many voices, some arguing and some chatting and one or two shouting. Unsettled to his core and repenting his fear, Lot crept up to a narrow opening. No door. Merely a curtain. Like a fissure leading into a charnel house.

In a corner of his mind he observed the shoddy workmanship and poor dye job; the crimson coloring did not reach every edge, bled, and showed darker splotches.

A central fire lent a smoky and sinister air to a large entrance room. Here several dusky figures lounged around the firepit, fighting chill night air while murmuring among themselves. But all talk ceased the moment Lot entered. Even at that instant, as he stepped through that poor curtain, his light withered and died.

"I seek my daughters. Two young women, dark hair done in Sheba style. Might have come in with a slender woman with hair kissed by fire."

That last description, of a red-haired skinny girl, caused a stir in the figure to his immediate right. A huge woman with unadorned hair, this figure caught Lot's eyes. He dashed over to her. "You have seen them. Tell me what floor and room, and I will speak no word of this to the magistrate."

Hardly a threat, really, considering magistrates all openly received bribes to overlook crimes. But mentioning the authorities still roused fear in simple folk.

She looked up. Whispered 'Second floor, southern corner room. Be careful, that Hashnah is a slippery serpent. She will do anything for her master."

Lot thanked the huge woman and sped deeper into the ramshackle structure, seeking stairs. Like a warren it was, hardly any light. Thunder rumbled. Inside, crumbling sounds erupted, as if quaking at the heavenly tumult. At last he found a stair ladder, tucked in a corner and lending hope despite its rickety wooden design. A couple figures lurked nearby in shadowy niches. Faces like twisted promises of violence.

Avoiding them best he could, Lot climbed one rung at a time. On the second floor he swung left, wishing his Seth light still shone. Darkness prevailed. It was like navigating his house in the middle of night when seeking the privy outdoors.

Only here enemies lurked at every doorway. Some domiciles boasted rough doors, closed, while others had only curtains. Lot heard many things emanating from those rooms. At one doorway a man whistled at him. Offered to have his way with Lot. He sped past, more concerned than ever. Even though this was merely a community house and not a flesh market or harem, it was still in the Gog district. Most who dwelt here were too poor to care what went on, or were in some way a part of the system.

At last he rounded the final hallway and reached the southwest corner room.

Blue-dyed curtain. Lot crept inside, reeled when he detected a whiff of foulness on the air. "Charity?" calling his eldest daughter. "Ammi?"

"Father?" a voice spoke, garbled and faint.

Lot strode deeper into the apartment, knocking over tools and bizarre whips and other unfamiliar items. A flickering oil lamp cast light upon the back wall. Lying bound on a shaggy rug, were his two daughters.

Upon seeing their father, they struggled to sit up.

Heart leaping and reeling simultaneously, Lot moved to step over a pile of reeking laundry, but stopped as Ammi's eyes widened and her mouth opened. Before she could speak, movement to his left made him twist round. But he was too slow.

A club flashed out toward his face.

Though Lot recoiled, the club still struck him a glancing blow. Pain flared in his temple. Staggering, he spun and caught himself on a divan, which crumbled beneath even his slight weight. Footsteps. Spotting Charity several feet away, bound and trembling, something stirred in the man and he found focus and strength.

Lot kicked out at his attacker's knee. A cracking sound accompanied a high shriek, and the figure crumpled to the floor. Scrambling to his feet, Lot snatched the fallen club. Held it over the writhing and moaning figure.

"Hashnah," he hissed, observing her long hair and skinny prone figure.

The temptation to lower the club and crush his enemy's face was indeed powerful. Lot was not a violent man. Had never physically harmed anyone. But this girl had deceived his daughters, stolen them, bound them like slaves, and . . . he feared what else. Had he arrived too late to preserve their chastity?

In the end his God stayed his hand. Not by physical restraint, but in the power of His Spirit upon the man. Lot willed not to harm one of the Lord's creatures.

After all, his own daughter's might be this very creature cringing beneath his gaze, had they been raised here in this city of sin instead of in the countryside, learning at righteous Abram's feet.

He flung the club away. Even as it clattered against straw bricks and third-rate wooden furniture, Lot scrambled to Charity and untied her bonds. Immediately on her liberation she embraced her father. Clinging to him, he was forced to pry her away. "I must free your sister." He moved to Ammi on his knees and tore off her scarlet bonds. The young woman also embraced her father, but unlike Charity, she did weep upon his shoulder.

With Ammi still clinging to him, and leaving the wicked little slaver Hashnah behind, Lot led his daughters out into the hall.

"Stay close and speak to no one."

By second watch they were free of the tenement and reached the spot where he had left Ebenezer. The old man was not there. Making a face, Lot drew his shivering daughters closer and pressed on against wind lash.

It was no easy task escaping the smothering cloister of Gog's district. In deep darkness, while assaulted by a heavy distracting fug so uncivilized it stirred angry feelings within, Lot trod back into the alley whence they had come. More than once he covered his daughters' eyes as he led them past unseemly goings-on. These nocturnal displays of lasciviousness were mere symptoms of the reason he chose to keep them home. Where they were, how he had found them—*that* was the prime reason.

He waited until they had at last reached home, that great bastion of light and peace amid viciousness, before asking them that burning question.

"Tell me true now, my darlings: did anyone befoul you?"

Ammi lowered her head, too shy to answer. Charity, two years older, shook hers. Her facial coloring was smudged by tears, and at the sight of this and the sound of her glad revelation, Lot's own eyes blurred. He put his head to theirs, each girl in turn, and kissed their crowns.

"Go inside now. Your mother is worried to death's edge."

"Thank you, Papa," Ammi hugged him tight. "Yes, thank the God of great Father Abram for you. We were so like dumb sheep to follow her—"

"Think not of that poor misguided girl tonight. You are home. We will rejoice, and discuss other matters later." After ushering them in, Lot looked over at his neighbor Ebenezer's house. He was not surprised to find his friend sitting upon a cedar settee there on his porch. A small bright red dot lit the night. Ebenezer, smoking hashish.

Lot strolled over there across a paving stone border.

"I know well what you would say," Ebenezer declared. "*A terrible friend. A cowardly wretch*, and you are right. I heard screams. Got done terrified near out my old skin! I rejoice with you that you recovered your daughters." The old man bowed and put two fingers to his lip, greasy white hairs dangling down his forehead. "Not many here are like you, Lot. We Sodomites are of Assyrian blood. Our gods speak no words to us, teach us no morals. Give us no laws but demands for flesh. I wish I were like you. But I am not."

Without a word, Lot turned and went back into his house.

It seemed there were even fewer godly men in Sodom than he had thought. Even just good men were in short supply.

From tonight, he knew of none.

But unknown to Lot, one *was* already heading toward Sodom, even in that terrible dark hour when he had risked his own life to save his daughters.

Chapter Three

Late that evening when everyone had at last fallen into slumber (Irith lay with the girls in the main room), Lot dropped to his knees beside his bed. After reuniting with them, Irith had placed balm of Gilead upon his temple. It now only throbbed. But his focus lay entirely upon his spiritual agony.

"Oh Lord," he cried out in a hushed murmur. "This city is filled with wickedness. Even the few decent men do nothing when they know to do right. Is that not as sin before Your holy eyes?" Lot groaned in his spirit. He had not the words nor the wisdom to rightly express the deepest sorrows of his heart. Felt helpless. Powerless to influence others in righteousness, to turn them from the error of their ways.

He closed his appeal with many words and cries of gratitude for delivering his daughters from evil and for safekeeping their chastity.

As he lay in bed later, Irith sleeping peacefully beside him, Lot longed once again for direct guidance from his Lord, the sort of powerful spiritual encounter Abram had recounted to him once. A vision in the night. God spoke to him. Promised him.

But for Lot, it was as if he could not hear God at all.

He knew to call upon the Possessor of heaven and earth. To think upon not only his own needs but the needs of others. To honor his Lord and Master with the first fruits of all his labor.

Beyond these good deeds and righteous lifestyle, he knew not what to do.

Several days passed.

In those first days which followed their harrowing ordeal, an unusual quietude descended upon their house. Neither girl spoke, except in murmurs, and only to their mother. After thanking Lot on their safe recovery and return home, they seemed to have developed a disliking for male company. Even Thomas, the small boy from several houses down, whom they loved to dress up in clothes and set him on the sheep for rides out back, they refused to see.

Perhaps young Thomas reminded them of Thomas' own father, a man with a foul tongue and heathen manners. Lot had noticed Thomas picking up these wicked habits.

When Lot came home at night from seeking work, they did not come rushing to the door like usual to greet him. He did miss that small joy sorely.

Another night followed another day.

Though morning arrived with a smeared red sunrise, barely visible between buildings, no answer had come from his prayers. Yet the Lord's face would shine upon Lot before the morning was out.

Being a Sabbath of rest the man did not go out seeking work. Instead, he went out to his small pasture behind their house very early. Quaint it was. Surrounded by abodes it may have been, but he had his own stonewall border within which he kept a single lamb and some hens.

He was out there sitting on the fence, petting his sheep, when a hubbub reached his ears. Sounded like a parade.

"What is going on—"

"Father!" Charity burst out into the yard. It was the first time he had heard the girls' voice clearly since before their abduction. "It is a procession of Father Abram and his house! He has come to visit, I think. Come on," she tugged on his arm and led him all through the house to the dirt street out front. He smiled to see her light up so.

Sure enough a caravan of camels approached. Instantly Lot recognized the banner and the unique purple coloring of their pageantry; it was his handiwork after all.

"Ah, go and tell your mother to prepare meal and begin baking cakes," he ordered Charity. As she sped back inside he called out, "Have her put in some raisins if we have any; Uncle Abram loves those. And put on your dress tunics, you and your sister both."

Sodom had a king, as did Gomorrah and Admah and Zeboiim (or rather, they all *once* had kings, until Chedorlaomer slaughtered them and ruled their cities). But no peasants or city folks ever saw him. The closest to royalty anyone in this street would ever see was Abram.

His uncle's humble chariot pulled up to Lot's abode just as Charity and Ammi and Irith arrived, shuffling out in their finest tunics, colored by Lot himself.

"I already had cakes rising, and there is unleavened bread and some mead," Irith said.

Lot took her hand and squeezed it. "You are the perfect partner. And you look as unto Mother Eve."

Camels clomped to a stop and complained. A tall man with a long gray beard tied with small lengths of hemp into a neat tail, emerged from the chariot. He was much older than Lot. Yet for all his years Abram wore an easy smile and was sturdy in build. Darker even than the weathered wood of his chariot, he was clearly a man of the fields, with strong-looking hands and the gaze and air of one who could speak to kings with authority.

"Father Abram!" the girls ran up to him first, using their endearing name for him.

The man embraced each in turn. "What beauties!" Raising his eyes to his nephew, Abram declared "The Lord shines upon you with such lovely blessings."

Lot both swelled with fatherly pride, and felt the sharp ribbing beneath those words; Abram knew as well as he that the Lord always did bless Lot, and that Lot often squandered these blessings. Abram was sagely telling him: *Do not disregard God's most precious gifts to you.*

"Uncle," he said, clutching forearms and then placing fingers to his lips to show respect. "I did not look to see you today, yet I believe the Lord has sent you as answer to prayer. How fares Aunt Sarai?"

As always, Abram was ebullient in his responses. Irith invited him in for cakes and figs and mead. The mighty man of God smiled at this but said "First, remember you my son, Ishmael?" He leaned down and whispered into Lot's ear: "It was Sarai's idea, the lying-with-her-handmaid thing. But see you do not bring it up when you behold her."

At a gesture, a dark boy on the verge of young manhood strolled up to Abram's side.

"Ishmael, you were in swaddling I believe, last time you met your kin, Lot. This is his wife, Irith, and his daughters Charity and Ammi."

On spotting the girls, a couple years older than himself, the boy's eyes widened and he turned shy, hiding behind his father.

"I brought figs and dates with sugar of the cane! Come, let us feast," Abram smacked his hands together and gestured for his son to follow the women into the house. But he remained behind with Lot. Once Ishmael had disappeared inside, a grand old lady emerged from the chariot, aided by the hand of a servant Lot barely recognized.

Slowly did this lady approach. Dressed in a fine red damask mantle and still blessed with a fair countenance despite advanced years, Sarai seemed healthy and all aglow.

It defied her graying hair.

When she stood beside her regal husband, looking small and happy, Lot beamed to behold her.

"Why Aunt, you look not your age. By now you must be nearly—"

"I know," Sarai interrupted with a titter, holding up a hand. "Say not my age before these young handmaids. They shall hear of it in Canaan. But indeed, the Lord has given me pleasure in my advanced days and blessed me." She laughed, a pure and hearty sound, sweet to hear. "Forgive me, I seem to laugh often of late."

Looking in awe up at Abram, who had taken Sarai's hand, Lot saw a great swelling pride which was clearly founded in gratitude to a God who gives liberally.

As always, Lot already felt better. Just being in the presence of one so faithful and joyful stirred in him the spirit of joy. Together they all enjoyed three measures of meal, cakes and sweetened figs and much else besides. Lot's larder would be nigh on empty by the time Abram's caravan took leave.

After they had feasted, the girls—with a helpful but shy Ishmael trailing along— brought food out to the servants, who had made camp along their street (much to the neighbors' annoyance no doubt).

Abram thanked Irith, calling her preparation a 'Meal for the ages!'

You old charmer, Lot mused.

He then led his revered uncle to a secluded area of the yard, and knelt at Abram's feet and crossed his legs. Then he waited for his elder to speak. Back in Ur of the Chaldeans, it had been customary to sit at elders feet to hear what they would say. A form of respect, which even those immoral Chaldeans performed.

"Many reports have reached my ears," Abram began, "informing me of the wickedness here, and in neighboring Gomorrah and the villages round about."

Lot hung his head.

Bending closer to him, Abram said in hushed tones of shock "Never have I heard such vile tidings, things which make one filthy just for hearing them. So I have come to take you home with me, again. You and all yours. Leave this place, my son. It is a den of robbers, murderers, extortioners, tax-defrauders and enactors of the basest perversions. Men openly engaging in sexual flights with other men. My own dear wife now leaves the room when one of my servants comes to give reports of these cities."

Through much of this declamation, Lot shook his head.

"I cannot leave."

"For the good Lord's sake, why remain in this viper's nest? Why subject your girls to such godless displays?"

Ebenezer's dogs barked, likely at some breezed motion of oilfat chapparal. Lot stood. "Uncle, if I leave Sodom, how will any here receive the truths and teachings of our Lord? How will they even *hear* these glad tidings?"

With those wise old eyes of his, Abram gazed at him.

Here was a man who had grown up in the last days of old Noah, who had himself spoken with ancient men who had in turn known Adam, the first man, in their early years. A living connection. A mighty prince. Even had Lot not been kin to Abram, he would still be in awe of the figure, and seek him out, for wisdom and emulation.

"Are there not temples? Surely there are priests who teach at least a small part of our Lord's truths, to a few faithful?"

Lot tittered bitterly at this.

"That is what I thought upon arriving here. But I have seen much and heard more of Sodom's priests. All are on the take, here. Worse they are than many notorious slayers of men! Some even—according to grapevine tales—closet themselves with boys."

The man kicked a stick aside. Felt like he was confessing his own transgressions here.

For a long space Abram remained silent, contemplative. When he spoke it was while standing and with a firm voice of authority.

"If it be so bad as all that, then leave this place and spare your daughters such a legacy."

Again Lot shook his head. "I cannot abandon these people. They are like sheep without a shepherd. Wolves at every turn and none defending against them, and the youth without even a godly example to follow."

It was here that Abram deduced a truth: "You punish yourself. That is why you remain here; you think you deserve to torture yourself by being among

51

these heathen uncircumcised sinners. But . . .
why? What guilt could you carry to inspire self-
scourging?"

Across the fence Lot spotted Ebenezer
shushing his mutts and bringing them inside.
Ebenezer caught his eye. Went back in.

"I was selfish," Lot confessed when Ebenezer
and the dogs were gone. "At the parting of the
ways at Bethel, you offered me the pick of land. I
chose the plains of Jordan, even pitching my tent
as far as this . . . *blessed* place. It was well-watered
everywhere. So I chose the better land. Huh." He
stomped on a fallen branch and snapped it. Bugs
buzzed out. "Almost from the moment we parted,
I struggled and found strife with everyone. Turned
out the land I claimed was owned by a Perizzite, a
very self-righteous and irritating man. When I
refused to take my livestock elsewhere, he set his
men to them. By the time I finally agreed to sell
them to this Perizzite, he had slaughtered half my
flock. Then I was forced to move into the city.

Upon that first day I ran into trouble. Conflict hounded me, even as street dogs attacked us and the stink of this place sunk into our clothes. I felt as old Cain must have, as though everyone's hand was against me. Sure enough they were, for that was when Chedorlaomer came and stood against the Five Kings. And then you came and saved me and mine. Now here you are, seeking to do the same again, for you are righteous and I am . . ."

"Think you that God punished you as he did Cain, that murderer of old?"

Lot nodded.

Taking his nephew by the shoulders, Abram smiled and declared, "That is not how the Lord works. Perhaps you *were* a bit selfish in choosing what you perceived to be better land. But the Lord blessed me in Canaan, a land flowing with milk and honey. And He has even promised to give all that land to my ancestors. So ye choosing *this* fertile valley was not entirely your doing. As for your suffering, have you not

53

considered it be more likely that the people of this place are simply exceedingly wicked and sinful against the Lord? They are a curse, like Cain, with their hand against every man and every man's hand against theirs. I reckon this Perizzite did not even have legal rights to that land."

Tears burned for release. Always it was wonderful and comforting to speak with a true man of God.

He nodded. Wiped his eyes. "Forsooth. I looked into it later, and that wicked Perizzite was just some bandit who happened to be sleeping out in those fields when I arrived. I might have struck back, and been justified in it."

Though he was sorely tempted to go back with his godly uncle, and though he knew it would be better for his wife and daughters, Lot could not shake a profound sense of duty to these Sodomites. Who would seek to help them were he to leave? Who would share God's truth and mercy and grace?

"I must stay," he at last declared. In the distance, someone screamed. Lot hardly noticed, so familiar had this clamor become. "It is a duty I do not feel I can shirk. However, my ways do not seem to be helping. Even my own neighbor, whom I thought a good man, forsook me in a terrible hour of need. Uncle, I know not how to help these people. What should I do?"

A slight breeze whisked the stink of feces through the yard. Abram wrinkled his nose.

Looking at his nephew, his own brother's only son and a child of God who was clearly weighed down with excessive concerns, this great man sighed. "If insist you do on remaining in this . . . filthy den, then I would suggest you sit at the gate."

This was an expression in Canaan, and one Lot had rarely heard.

"Sit at the gate?"

Leading him back toward the house, Abram nodded. "It means you sit at the entrance of a city where business is transacted, and seek to spiritually guide those who enter. Greet them with the light of our Lord, with the oil of gladness which He has given to those of us who know Him. It also means you sit as judge of those *within* the gates of this city. To point out their sins."

Lot stroked his beard. "Oh, I am certain that will go over well with these Sodomites."

A chuckle from Abram. "Yes, well, many will doubtless fault you for it. But some few might just—by the grace of our God—receive your pronouncements as seeds in the good ground. Plant them, and mayhap God will water them. Of course, sitting at the gates will earn you many enemies. If serious you are about staying and doing the Lord's work, and if you have hope the Lord shall respond and bless your works, then you might try this old method."

Chill winds brought more rank gusts flitting across their noses. So the men went inside.

Here the aroma of cakes and cinnamon bread relieved them. Lot thanked his uncle for guidance, agreeing upon the spot that he would try to sit at the gate.

On the morrow he shared with Abram his recent trial in Gog's district. About Hashnah.

Irith also spoke with Sarai of Lot's trouble with his fellow worker, Ham.

In exchange, and by way of encouraging Lot that God often dealt with the wicked in strange and unexpected ways, Abram informed him to "One day take a trip out to the asphalt pits in the Valley of Siddim. There you will see what is the end of kings who promote wickedness. Remember, we serve a mighty God. And when we seek Him truly and daily, with our whole heart, the Lord always triumphs in our lives." A firm clap on the back followed this. "Take heart, Lot. I know not the fate of Sodom, but if you seek the Lord always, and trust Him, then He will be to you a strong tower in the days of calamity."

When Abram loaded up his caravan two days hence, Lot caught sight of two people he recognized, who had not been part of the caravan on arriving.

Ham, who was attached by ropes to the rearmost cart; and Hashnah, who sat bound in the same, still bruised. That slippery snake looked terrified.

"Strange and unexpected ways, indeed," Lot grinned and waved goodbye.

It would be a few weeks before he saw the fruits of his 'sits in the gate'. A lesser man might have quit afterwards. Lot, however, was determined not to let even such personal disappointment as that deter him from honoring his God before all people.

Chapter Four

His period of punishment fulfilled, Lot returned to work.

On the first day of the following week, after leaving his labors at Evil-Hadad's, he traversed Sodom's grimy streets to arrive at its western gate.

He was forced to endure only a single potentially dangerous encounter; Nahab had spotted him on Jezeb Street and shadowed Lot for the next two. Thinking the man might be in the mood for violence, Lot had made sure to keep near to Chedorlaomer's soldiers. Those men were not righteous. But they had a reputation for quelling any tussles not instigated by themselves.

Lacking opportunity, Nahab eventually lost interest.

Denizens flowed in and out of the gates of Sodom, along with visitors, mostly Gomorrahians doing daily business or trade or delivering and receiving goods.

The gates themselves were cast bronze. A rarity, the metal doors had once been a wonder of the east, but had since dulled and were rarely ever closed now.

Taking up a spot at the opening of the right-side gateway, where he would be easily seen and heard, Lot settled in for his work.

A bench here sloppily made of almug wood reinforced with rusted iron nails, supported both him and his woolen bag, out of which he retrieved a papyrus slab of Hebraic writing. It might have been in Babylonian for all these Sodomites knew. Few could read his native tongue, and their own did not even have a written system.

But he had asked for this small recording of the words of Enoch, from Abram. Hoping it would legitimize his own spiritual exhortations and admonitions.

Certainly it must have been hard for Uncle Abram to give up such a priceless family heirloom. Everyone knew it was Enoch who had devised the art of writing. Few however realized this sample was scrolled by Enoch himself. Lot looked upon this precious gift as Abram's blessing on his new endeavor. A holy sacrifice.

For a time he sat there silently reading old words of a righteous ancestor, who had walked with God, and then was not.

Enoch's words, a testimony and—according to legend—sourced from his long devoted prayers and communion (his 'walk') with the Lord Himself, described a world before the Flood. A world of simple purity. Pure grace. No civilization, no governments.

Then it gave an account of a disturbing change; it went on to define the exact forms of wickedness which grew out of the corruption unleashed by Cain, indulged in by almost the whole earth by the time of Noah, and which manifested in all manner of desire, hatred, self-will, and disregard for the holy.

Sitting there at the gates of Sodom, listening to various harsh words slung back and forth, and witnessing the detestable practices of slave trade and servitude and open bribery, Lot had no trouble picturing the days of Noah, when all the thoughts of man were evil continually—or imagining how that righteous man himself must have felt, dwelling amid such fornicating unholy populaces.

Following a prayer seeking the Lord's guidance and beseeching Him for boldness, Lot opened his mouth and began to read aloud.

It was another cloudless day. No breeze. Sweat built, both from heat and nerves.

The text was in Middle Hebraic, yet Lot translated easily to their common tongue.

"What the Lord of Heaven puts in their hearts, let not men reject. His righteousness is offered unto all, to give strength to stand and fight when the enemy enters in. If we embrace His offer, we have God. If we embrace it not, we have not God. Our strength will not suffice, and we will fall to our enemy."

In time he became absorbed in the encouraging words and wise warnings, and forgot to be nervous. Forgot even his physical discomfort. His natural bashfulness.

For the first time, Lot publicly shared the truths upon which he had been raised. To display his joy and gladness in this knowledge. To bring forth the light in which he dwelt. It made him want to shout with crystalline delight into the heady mood and sweltering air of Sodom.

In this spiritual state, Lot did not realize a small crowd had gathered at the gates.

The cold deformed shadows they cast made him look up. Had they been listening? Learning, perhaps? *Should I go on?* he wondered.

"What you spouting off there?" one of the figures croaked.

Before Lot could answer, and even as he gauged the malevolent temper of this brooding mob, another quipped: "On about his foreign god again, is my reckoning."

"I only seek to help you onto a righteous path," Lot tried, beginning to tremble. "It is clear Sodom has become a cesspit of transgressions and corruption. But we need not remain on such a path—"

"What is tansgerression?"

"Transgression," he corrected. "It means sin. Unrighteous deeds requiring an offering to God above. The slave trade is a major transgression, or sin. Sacrificing newborns to the fires of Ba'al is certainly another. Just vile—"

"Them sacrifices keeps Ba'al satisfied, elsewise we be flooded by an overrun Jordan."

Of course Lot had often heard this claim before. It baffled him. As if the mass slaughter of newborns had anything to do with weather. There was simply no excuse. Yet even otherwise decent people like Ebenezer accepted this deplorable practice as 'something others do, and who am I to stop their beliefs?'

"Perhaps if we were to put off some of our practices which are . . . contrary to the design of the God of heaven, like men leaving the natural use of the woman and burning in lust for—"

"Who made ye judge over us, outsider? Go back to your mudslop homeland."

"Yeah, nobody here wants your foreign God with all His laws! Get out, ye judging pilgrim!"

With so many voices vehemently assaulting him, and many in the mob beginning to spit on him, Lot knew they would soon rile themselves into a frenzy. Physical violence would ensue. He collected his written tablet of papyrus and stalked off into the city. Head down, cowed and fearful with a mob shouting at his back.

Rain pattered and plinked against roughshod streets. By the time Lot turned down onto his own lane, Sodom was being hammered by rain.

Soaked and shivering, he was greeted by Ammi, who called for her mother. While waiting for Irith to finish up whatever enterprise she was engaged in, Ammi helped her father out of his cloak. Thunder rumbled, shaking dust loose and clattering shutters in their clay slides. "Where have you been?" the girl asked, taking the papyrus and carefully setting it upon a second-hand bureau from Admah.

Lot sighed as he shrugged out of his linen garment top. He wondered absently why Ammi was so comfortable seeing him half-disrobed. Until the turning of her seventeenth year last month, she had always proven a shy girl, giggling at any young man passing by outside, even tittering and turning aside when she had seen Ebenezer's dogs coupling.

"With your Uncle Abram's blessing, I have begun sitting at the gates."

Now at last Ammi displayed some proper bashfulness; she inhaled and covered her mouth.

"You were out there . . . sitting in judgment of these Sodomites? But that is—"

"A fool's move?"

"I was to say it is a brave and righteous thing to do. So it seems to me."

To Lot's shock the girl now threw her arms around him, embracing him. Her soft cheek nestled against the course dark hair of his chest. He nudged her away to arm's length. "What is the meaning of this?"

Looking up into his eyes, his younger daughter said in a broken voice "I am proud of you. But . . . also I fear for you. They will not look to like your sitting in judgment of them."

Irith arrived with a dry cloth. Lot took it and smiled, wiping his torso. "No indeed. They did gather and yell and some even spat. Yet . . . and yet there was one who did not. A small man. Now I think of it, I saw him, this small man listening as I read the words of our ancient kin, good Enoch. Perhaps this man—"

"Perhaps he will receive your words and turn to our God?"

Though Ammi seemed quite taken with the notion, romanticizing it as young women so often do, Irith was giving Lot a decidedly stern expression. Her crossed arms also spoke clearly. He read a warning in her look. He heard a future *talking to* in it.

Irith confirmed this when she scolded Ammi. "Now look, you have gotten water all over, soaking into the floor. Take these to the mud room and hang them. Go on, little bird."

"Thank you, dear," Lot called to Ammi as she snatched up his tunic and under linen.

"Well come then," said Irith, "to bedroom with you. Catch an ill you shall, standing there all naked—and in front of our girls. What am I to do with you? You know they are at that age?"

"What age is that?" Lot asked as they strolled through a narrow cedar-lined hallway into their room. Using a flintstone, Irith lit a Seth light to ward off gloom.

Setting hands to hips and gazing at him with a sideways smile, Irith said "The age, my dear, when they start to notice menfolk."

Thinking of this, Lot realized it explained quite a bit of behavior from Ammi and Charity of late. He chuckled. "Indeed? Well my dear, I shall seek to keep from getting rained upon."

"I should more hope you seek not to go sit at the gate again," helping him disrobe.

Lot had been musing on this very subject. He did not like confrontation. These Sodomites were stuck in their wicked ways, and mostly he did not believe any effort could dislodge them from their self-wrought path to Sheol. Yet for all his doubting heart, Lot also longed to be of use to his God—even if the result was seemingly hopeless. If even one man heeded his warnings and exhortations to turn from the error of his ways, then all the persecution would be worth it.

"If you would join me, we shall pray on it. Let the God of my father's tell us what He wills us to do. For I know not."

He did not like sharing with his wife the fact that he did not know what to do.

But never did he regret leaning on the everlasting arms for guidance.

From the peace which followed their nightly prayer together, even Irith—despite her objections and feelings on the matter—had to accept that the Lord's will was clear: Lot was to continue 'sitting in the gate' of Sodom.

Someone had to do it. This city—and her twin, Gomorrah—were begging for divine judgment. Better Lot should dole it out in words, than the Lord by His terrible swift sword.

Chapter Five

It so happened on the first day of the following week, in that month of Iyyar, as soon as Lot returned from another disappointing session at Sodom's gates, that he found himself facing yet another trial of faith.

His wife was not at home.

When he asked the girls where she had gone, they shrugged. "Mother said she was visiting a friend. Said if you could spend time away from home, not working, so could she."

"Oh Lord," he prayed later, "are You testing me with this? Am I not serving Your will?"

His matrimonial concerns would have to wait, however. The city crier and his attendants walked by, declaring a citywide vote to be taken on the morrow. It came about every so often, this *alleged* opportunity for citizenry to take part in its government.

Lot was outside on the clay listening when he noticed Ebenezer on his porch.

Something prompted him to stroll over to his neighbor. The man seemed ready to turn and flee into his house, but then stopped and nodded as Lot approached. Gesturing at the receding crier, Ebenezer chortled "How kind of our rulers to pretend we have any say in what goes on here."

"Maybe this year they will hear our voices and retract their taxation and work dictates and enforced child labor donkey turds," Lot replied with a dismissive sneer.

They shared a jaded grin.

It was a sad truth that despite its everchanging governance, Sodom never improved. Oh, the rulers often pretended to give its citizenry opportunity to voice their will, but everyone knew it was a sham. The city meetings, where everyone shouted for a rescinding of oppressive measures, always resulted in the same régime claims: 'We represent your will, we have heard you, and the majority clearly want this, that, and the other to continue.'

"Listen, Lot—"

"No need," Lot interrupted. "I understand." And he did. He understood fear as well as Ebenezer, as well as any man in Sodom. But his fear of his God outshone all other types. His fear of disappointing his Maker trumped physical fear.

"Did you happen to see which way Irith went?"

With a nod, Ebenezer pointed, then grabbed his goat skin bottle and headed out to his evening job.

Lot did not like the doleful manner in which Ebenezer had nodded and gestured. The only 'friends' Irith could boast in east Sodom were a pair of Wager Ladies, who tossed coin at Shem's Gambling House. She had developed a taste for that wicked practice when they first arrived here, and those seemingly kind generous women had fronted Irith a few silver shekels to wager.

Much prayer and temple-attending and confessions it had taken to free her from that sin.

Lot had thought his wife was done with gambling.

73

Perhaps his long absences and the personal threats at their own home had taken its toll on her mind, and now she sought escape from growing persecution and social exclusion in passing excitement?

He checked their clay jar, kept in an alcove in their bedroom closet, behind a heavy bearskin cloak.

At the sight, he groaned. It was definitely light several coins.

What was a man to do amid all this rot and corruption, so deep imbedded in the city that it infected even its few good inhabitants?

He grabbed his plain wool cloak (the ones he had dyed drew too much attention) and a small bronze dagger, and stormed toward the front door. "Girls! I have to go fetch your mother. Remember ye to clean the sheepfold. I shall be back before dark." He hoped.

A small soft hand caught his at the stout cedar door. At that exact moment thunderheads rumbled, shaking loose clouds of dust from fixtures around the abode.

Charity looked up into her father's eyes. Hers shone stunning hazel, catching the flame from a nearby rushlight. "You will leave us here, alone? What are we to do if something happens to both of you? No one to take us in! It would take weeks to contact Father Abram. By then we could be taken by another slaver!"

"She is right, father," Ammi added, entering from the kitchen area.

"I must bring her back, she has . . . your mother has fallen into her old ways. She is not thinking or acting in a godly manner."

Another heavenly rumble made them all start.

"You hear that?" asked Charity. "That storm is almost upon us, and it brings great darkness with it. How will you find your way? It is dangerous out on those streets. You always say so, and now we know you were right, because of what happened to us."

Lot set his bag down and drew his hands down his face. They still possessed lingering patches of cerulean dye.

"It will be fine. I brought you two back, did I not?"

The girls traded a look. Finally, when Charity spoke, it was with a shaky voice but firm words: "We will *not* be left alone in this city. We are coming with you to find Mother."

Never had they defied him before; Lot did not sense any disregard for his paternal authority here, only a profound fear and perhaps a sense of duty.

"Hmm," he grumped. "You have spent too much time with your Uncle Abram; you are becoming just as mule headed as he! But come if you must. If I have to worry about you two as well, then you might as well be with me." He turned to head out as they collected their blue veils, but then whipped back around and pointed a finger at each daughter in turn. "You will mind my every word, and you will not leave my side for anything!"

Lord protect us from abominable men, Lot prayed upon leaving his door.

After tying his sandals on, he placed the stile into its slot, which should deter any potential break-ins. So much easier had it been when traveling with Abram. Back then he had a covered chariot. Not kingly, but convenient, offering protection against weather, and there had always been a sense of superiority.

On splashing through puddles, soaking his sandals and muddying the hem of his garment, Lot supposed that was the point of humbling him. Perhaps God had not appreciated Lot's growing pride back then.

The girls kept hard by him, even cowering during thunderclaps, only to giggle nervously afterward at themselves.

There is no reason to suspect Irith is in immediate danger, he thought.

Except there *was* reason. There were several frightening, impending reasons, in fact. Irith might gamble herself into debt. Sodom's wagering places did not accept any excuse. If she did win, Irith might very well be followed out into Sodom's rank alleys and attacked for her winnings, or even accosted in its main avenues. Crime in this sinful city was by now almost proudly committed in broad daylight.

That was simply the random crooks.

Organized criminals and city officials were one the same.

That is what happens when sin is made law by corrupt men in authority, Lot understood, and his shoulders sagged at this awful thought.

As rain pelted them, seeping past the cheapness of their cloaks and chilling their flesh, Lot reflected on how far from his God these people and its leaders had wandered, and he understood just how profound a weight he had been lugging around. Sure as God lived, he knew it had descended upon him since moving into the battered rotten heart of Sodom. It had even altered his physical posture, did this spiritual weight. He stooped now.

Stooped he may be, yet still blessed the man was with two beautiful pure daughters; he drew them close to his side, huddling as they braved the storm.

Most folks were either at work or shut up in their abodes.

Still, there were those who milled about, never ones to let a storm keep them from their harlotries or carousing or wagering or bag-picking.

Just past city center, Ammi suddenly stopped, tugging on Lot's arm.

"What?" fearing the worst.

The girl pointed overhead at a brooding heavens lit by some ghastly backdrop. "It looks on fire," she declared in awe.

"What is it, father?" Charity asked, clutching onto his right arm.

Rumbling erupted. It seemed to be coming from directly above *and* all around; Lot even felt it shivering inside his chest. "Just a strange lightning in the heavens. Come."

Most streets in Sodom were dirt or lightly sprinkled with pebbles, with a few wider avenues being coated with some manner of fine sandy bricks, only with a green tint.

But not this one.

The further they trod the sloppier became their lane. So Lot led them down alleys in a circuitous route. These were reeking cesspools, but tended to have bricked culverts, channels they could straddle without slopping through mud.

In the last alley before opening onto the avenue with Shem's Gambling House, they stumbled onto a nightmare scene.

Lot immediately recognized the situation. He had heard of such goings on. But never had he witnessed this specific depravity, and it shook loose some moral temper inside, an inner fervent spirit which, upon the average, he did not express outwardly.

"Go now, hide thee hence behind those crates," Lot ordered his daughters, and then he leaped toward the scene. A man lurked in that corner beneath a low overhang, protected from rain—and from onlookers from the street. From the alley, however, Lot saw this man's sin plain as day.

"Take your hands off the boychild."

Instantly the man ceased his sexual assault against the boy. Though caught in his debauchery, he did not immediately retrieve his linens, but merely turned an evil eye onto Lot without releasing the boy. "Go mind thine own affairs, *meddler*, and leave me to mine."

Lightning briefly lit up the child. Tears ran tracks down bespattered cheeks, and fear displayed itself in trembling little limbs.

"This *is* my affair, *Sodomite*," Lot returned with more heat than he had ever felt.

With an annoyed sigh, the man bent down to collect his linen underthings. As he was doing this, Lot retrieved a loose piece of broken brick he had noticed and, gesturing silently for the boy to duck, he did sling it at the sinner. It struck his head with a thunk and clattered to the alley floor. The man staggered forward. On his face now, and reeling from the blow, he did not see Lot dart forward and snatch the boy from his dark corner.

Lot wanted to hurt the man worse. He would have liked to give him a lesson. He wished to turn him toward the Lord, to drive such a beast to repentance.

Instead, he called the girls forward (they were already helping the child back into his filthy mantle), and ushered them toward the end of the alley where flickering light beckoned. Soon as they reached the end, they turned right and slowed. Shem's Gambling House rose to the height of four men before them.

In half light, Lot saw for the first time a dark crescent upon the nape of the boychild's neck. A slavers brand.

I should go back there, finish that heathen off.

It was not a righteous thought, and anyway Lot had his girls in tow and a boychild and his wife in need of either saving or a swift hand of discipline.

There were outposts scattered across Sodom and its sister cities. Places of supposed refuge, run by magistrates, sometimes a judge, who were meant to adjudicate local altercations and take in the injured and attacked, the widowed and orphaned. But like all institutions in Sodom, their purpose had been corrupted. Because those running these places had become corrupted. Rotten to the core. They would sell their parents or their children if it brought in a few gold salt tablets.

So for now, he had the girls keep the boy at hand.

A murderous thunderclap trembled over Sodom. Many of the revelers at Shem's uttered surprised shrieks, along with Lot's youth.

Shem's Gambling House proved to be an enormous tent, tall as the surrounding structures, a patchwork of thick hides specially treated and never properly dried, making it resilient to common fire. A vast crowd of subjects crushed each other. Everyone shouting their bets or declaring treachery from their loss.

They were soaked through by now. Against their protestations, Lot tucked the children into a cozy niche beside a bread vendor's carriage. Its awning would keep them dry.

With throngs jostling him, stink of their sweat permeating even a fine aroma of fresh rain, Lot spent a good while searching for his wife, eventually finding her casting lots at a table. Her hair hung like wet straw outside her veil. As displayed above her sagging veil, her eye paint dripped in dark trails. Wild eyes. She looked a woman possessed.

"Pardon me," Lot said, shoving his way to her. "Irith?" taking her by the shoulder.

"What?" without looking at him, she cast a lot. Lost. "You sunny serpent! Look what ye made me lose!" Only then did she turn to her husband; it still took a moment before she seemed to recognize him. "Lot? What—"

"It is past time to leave this place, wife." Leaving no room for discussion.

Yet for all his husbandly sternness, Lot found his wife unresponsive. She shrugged out of his grasp and, listening to those surrounding the table as they urged her to cast again, Irith resumed her strange addiction. Her veil hung loose. A disgrace she seemed not to notice.

His subsequent attempts proved just as fruitless, Lot's voice often conquered by thunder or his ministrations marred by interlopers demanding he leave the lady alone.

Finally, employing his skill of judging the temper of the crowd (this one as being on verge of violence in their almost drugged state), he returned to his daughters.

"Where is Mother?" they shook in fear at the sight of him, alone.

Dejected was becoming his normal state.

He plopped down onto the broken stone wall beside his children. The boy was shivering. Lot removed his mantle, took off his linen vest and wrapped that dry piece around the boy, then pulled his tunic back on. "Hardly does she behave now as your Mother. She will not listen. She—"

"Let us go and try?" Ammi suggested. "Yes, perchance Mother shall heed us," Charity offered.

He sighed. Told them where she was and warned them not to upset anyone. "Any trouble, you shout for me. And keep your veils up tight." He helped Ammi with hers.

For most of the time they were gone, the man prayed.

When he opened his eyes, he saw that the boy was looking up at him. At least he was no longer crying or trembling. "Did you . . . do you ever pray?"

The boy shook his head. Seemed to indicate 'prayer' as a mystery.

"Have you never seen a man pray?" As soon as he spoke these words, Lot realized he should not be surprised, considering the boys' servitude and where he had been raised.

"When you pray, you honor our Creator and Deliverer. You show the Lord of all creation that you consider yourself His servant and that you seek His will in your life. You may ask anything. You can tell the Lord anything, and He never hurts you or makes you feel bad in any way. In prayer, we reach into something beyond ourselves, beyond these weak tents," Lot placed three fingers against his forehead, the sign of the body as a tent. "We reach into the divine, and find help, and guidance, and even correction when necessary. Often the Lord will intervene on our behalf, and keep us safe from the enemy—if in His own peculiar ways."

The boy took all this in without a word.

Lot wondered if he had explained it well enough to plant a seed. He hoped he had. Perhaps that was where he was going wrong with his gate sittings; the men and women of Sodom were so set in their ways, so jaded and corrupt, that nothing good could reach through their hardened shells of sinfulness. But children . . . maybe that was the hope for Sodom.

Then again, many a disturbing time had he witnessed Sodom's youth engaging in the very depravity of their parents. Raised from the cradle in the ways of sin.

As the boy huddled beneath his tunic, Lot noticed a strange scar on his right wrist. No, not a scar. Another brand. One upon his neck claiming him as property. One upon his wrist to designate his 'owner'.

He did not know the group or individual the brand named. But that seared raised flesh instantly revealed two facts: the boy had been suffering for some time before Lot stumbled on him in that alley; and someone would come looking for him—and those who took him.

In that darkling moment Lot's own personal fears and concerns evaporated, like water in a clay jar left out in summer sun.

Branded a slave. This poor child has endured nightmares, perhaps for his whole life. Why do I whine about my own struggles to righteous Abram? I did wrong and suffer. This boy . . . he never did anything wrong, and he has suffered infinitely worse, for his entire life.

He had to get the boy out. Out of this servitude. Out of Sodom.

While contemplating these matters, his girls emerged from Shem's huge tent, with Irith in tow. His wife had clearly been weeping.

Irith's head hung low. Lot knew she was deep in shame.

The Lord must have answered his prayers, giving the girls the precise words they needed to convince their mother to come home. And home they went. The storm drenched them all, but none seemed to notice,

so relieved to reach the homeplace safely.
Everyone returned—and with a child rescued from
the Sodom child trafficking market.

On the morrow, Lot's real work commenced.
In addition to helping his wife withdraw from her
addiction, and finding a way to get the child out of
Sodom and safely into the care of his uncle, Lot
also felt the Lord was laying it upon his heart to sit
in the gate again.

It was as if he were being pulled, drawn
toward Sodom's entrance. As if his life and more
depended upon his being there.

Chapter Six

Every summer there was a hiatus at Evil-Hadad's. Six weeks of no work.

All the flocks sheared. All wool dyed or sold or parceled. Time was needed for the sheep to regrow their coats.

Of course, everyone knew the truth. Evil-Hadad took weeks off every summer to haggle deals with the Queen down in Sheba. Many rumors flew. He was the Queen's harlot-master. Her plaything. He stole from her. He was in debt to her.

Though it always meant even harder times at home (Irith had to spread their few saved coins real thin, much like they had to thin their mead down to make it last—for visitors, as Lot did not partake), Lot realized it offered a prime opportunity.

The morning following their dark night (which commenced the 6 week hiatus), Lot gathered everyone—including the boy, who had at last whispered his name of Joshua to Ammi—into the open room.

Gloom hung heavy. Wood still swelled and stank from last night's rain. Rainfall always conjured waste smells from public and private waste rooms.

Yet for all their weariness and gloominess, Lot beamed. He finally felt led of God. "I am going to take little Joshua out of Sodom today." Turning eyes to the boy, he continued: "I will take you to my uncle in Canaan. He is a great and good man, a prince among men. He has many servants, but they are not slaves. No brands." He added that last part after seeing Joshua recoil and cover his hand at the mention of servants. Ammi pulled him in a tight embrace.

"His servants are born in his house, and he treats them as family."

"Father Abram is very rich," Charity said by way of encouragement. Her softer, enthusiastic voice, along with Ammi's comforting arms, seemed to soothe the child. "You will have dry shelter, safety from raiders—even the Chaldeans dare not molest the people of Father Abram. And there is much food. Raisins baked in cakes and figs and rolls and fresh greens."

Lot nodded. "Indeed, and you will have your own section of a large tent, likely."

Taking the girls aside, Lot instructed them in making sure their mother drank plenty of water, and some mead, and he told them "Make no mention of her gambling sins. Right now she needs our love only."

"She was trying to make coin for the hiatus, right father?" Ammi asked.

He nodded. "It is the man's duty to provide for his family. Our father Adam taught us this. The woman keeps the home from falling apart. A virtuous wife is worth far more than rubies. Her husband trusts her, for she works in wool and flax, brings in the food and rises early to prepare for her household. She fuels the lamps and makes wise purchases. Your mother is all these things. She has only wandered off a bit, like our lamb does so on occasion."

No one mistreated Lot and Joshua as they trekked through Sodom's sodden lanes.

Last night's torrent had flooded the city's poorly designed sewage system, so that in addition to Sodom's usual reek, now a fug of human filth lingered everywhere. Even fresh aromas of bakeries failed to quench this ungodly stink. Flies buzzed everywhere like a constant ache in the head, while street dogs licked blood from alleys where spoiled meat and bones had been tossed.

Beside Lot, Joshua ambled along with seeming eagerness plagued by fear. Head scanning every direction from beneath the mantle Lot had given him.

Their only bump on the path out of Sodom was at its gates—the very same he had chosen to begin his most difficult work for God. Here, while trying to pass the posted centurion and a loud businessman settling debts, Lot was identified.

"I know you," spat Chedorlaomer's soldier. "Thou art the one who made himself judge over us. The foreigner."

Joshua took and squeezed Lot's hand.

"I oft do sit here at the gate, sharing my hope and—"

"Judging us, more like," interrupted a grimy Sodomite who must have reminded Joshua of his master, for the boy suddenly cringed and sought refuge behind Lot.

Centurions were known for their curiosity, often hired for their inquisitive minds and keen eyes. This one apparently more than most. Observing Joshua's response, he looked over at the one who had spoken.

"Know ye that sniveling scrap?"

A head shake. Followed by a leering grin of yellow teeth. "Mayhap I like to, though. How much for the lad, judge?"

Despite all the wickedness Lot had witnessed over his years in this city, never had he considered others might view him as partaker in their iniquities. Yet here was a sinner, either slaver or flesh peddler or child fondler, who thought Lot would help him in his beastly yearnings.

"He is a child of God. His body and soul are not for sale." He knew almost upon the instant that they would not handle this declaration well.

As the centurion and beastly man glowered at Lot, their numbers soon swelled with other lookers-on who had been half listening. Temper stirred among this burgeoning mob. Lot's time in Sodom had honed his ability to read a crowd. Another few minutes and they would stir their own pot into a revolting stew of violence.

It was simply something many liked to do— stir up the masses against individuals, or against certain parties and groups.

Still keeping the hooded and cloaked Joshua at his back, Lot backed away from them. They followed. Hissing and spitting, denouncing and carousing; some were clearly drunk with wine. The gate stood tall, dull but impassibly solid, a foreboding twenty feet away. What could he do to escape? No allies. No weapons. You could not speak sense into mindless mobs.

Like the gentle cooing of a single dove amid a murder of crows, came the soothing music of psaltery.

A tune like a babbling brook. It stole the wind right out of their sails, and as everyone looked around in search of this strange melodic interloper, Lot broke from his trance and led the boy out from among the crowd, all the way through those great and terrible gates.

Free air.

Almost on the moment they stepped upon worn sloppy earth outside those gates, Lot breathed easier and freer than he had for several years.

Beside him, Joshua kept glancing back. But after passing the brick sphinx outside the gate, with

Sodom—and all its stink and oppressiveness—dwindling behind, he let go Lot's hand and lowered his mantle. Something akin to a smile flittered across the boys' face. Hot wind licked at them as they trod onward.

Far as Lot was concerned, it was like God kissing them a blessing.

Following two days' march and most of a third night, they spotted a constellation of lights like beacons upon a hill, and Lot knew they had reached Uncle Abram's at last.

Though his arrival was a surprise, and his young company an even greater wonder, Lot was welcomed with great love and treated as a beloved—if prodigal—son. Aunt Sarai insisted he and the boy spend the evening in her tent in place of she and Abram. It was a fine abode fit for nobility. Spacious. Even smelled divine, some form of foreign incense perhaps. Anise. Cinnamon. Frankincense, mayhap.

Countless stars twinkled in vast heavens. Lot rarely saw them anymore; there were always hundreds of open firepits and ovens or rushlights blazing in Sodom every hour of every night, darkening their vision of the Lord's celestial art.

Delicacies he tried here, but for both Lot and Joshua, the former sex slave, they proved too rich for the palette. Lot asked for some millet and grapes. Enjoyed some date wine.

When he gave a sip of it to the boy, Joshua coughed and smacked his lips.

Both laughed.

A pleasant night sleep followed. No stray dogs barking endlessly. No interruptions from quarreling neighbors shouting. No mysterious banging noises from roving bands of thugs.

In the morning for the first time in years, Lot beheld the richness in foliage and produce and vistas and even people Canaan boasted. It truly was a land *flowing with milk and honey.*

A perfect place, thought he, for young Joshua to grow up in. And under the tutelage and spiritual example of Abram, the boy was sure to grow strong in the God of all creation. This thought, this revelation, filled Lot with waves of gratitude and gladness; the Lord had finally used him to bless another, to lead a fellow human to grace.

That was the hope upon which he had lain his head last night, and the peace which led him on that afternoon.

Following a prayer with Abram, and a strange encounter with Aunt Sarai (she positively glowed, as if she had received the greatest news), he took leave of his relatives and, now laden with peace and hope, headed for Mount Sodom, quite a hike from here.

Clopping footfalls caught him up. Lot turned. Speeding his way was Joshua.

The boy fell upon him. A surprisingly strong embrace it was for one so small and emaciated.

When he held the child back from him, Lot saw wetness upon those cheeks. And a smile.

He nodded, acknowledging the silent gratitude. "You heed Abram, and God's favor will shine upon you. Go on now. I must be off."

A long quiet hike followed this satisfying separation.

Green hills outside Canaan provided plenty of fertile landscapes and fowl with exotic plumage and creatures of the field for Lot to enjoy. Often along the trek he inhaled deeply. Air so pure you could not detect even a whiff of filth. When a breeze picked up, he feared it might carry some of that old familiar stink, but instead it brought to his oft-offended nose the aroma of lilac.

This aided in keeping his spirit at peace.

It was in this unusual state that the following day Lot at last passed through terebinth foliage and hiked up to Mount Sodom. Several times had he trekked up here for prayer, for pilgrimage and sweet repose from the city's incessant racket and distractions. There were in this area and all around the mountains near Zoar, standing stones and dolmens. These had been associated with Ba'al and Marduk, long ago, and Lot bypassed them without so much as raising his eyes to their offensiveness.

A long time ago someone had boldly erected an altar not far east of these altars to false gods. It was a crude thing, really, this dais. One flat obsidian raised atop a half-buried stone. But the altarpiece did boast letters carved into its topside, writing very similar to those upon the Enoch papyrus.

Lot made out parts of the legible areas, surmising it read: **Jehovah Jirah.**

THE LORD WHO PROVIDES.

Normally he stopped here to pray, but something in his spirit led him upward. He climbed until he reached an open promontory. Spread out in misty morning distance, looking small and busy, lay the cities of Sodom and Gomorrah, and like a speck of dust further still was Arnon and what must be its river gorge, with that great blot being the Sea of Salt.

But he could not be sure.

After killing a pigeon, he returned to the altar and, removing his sandals, used a bronze blade to slice its neck and drip its blood upon the altarpiece.

Lot was no priest, but Abram *had* consecrated him back in Bethel, so that offering sacrifices upon an altar was considered an acceptable practice by him.

As blood slithered across a jagged channel in the stone's face, he knelt and prayed.

"I thank you Lord for employing me, using my wife's weakness to lead us to that poor child in the alley. For helping us past Sodom's gate. I know not who played that music—if You did send a man or angel—but through it You provided escape for us. Oh, thank you, Jehovah Jirah! Thank you for helping me bring Joshua safely out of that den of thieves and to my uncle; I know Abram is Your chosen servant and that you will bless the boy through him."

As he went on, Lot confessed his own sins—especially his sin of unbelief.

For the man had not believed the Lord could use him to save others. Now he knew that He could. He did pray for some time, until he had lingered so long unmoving that birds settled in the area and hopped and sang, and critters shuffled across pebbles nearby, and he even heard the ululating call of an ibex.

At last the Lord Himself seemed to call an end to the prayer, for Lot heard his name.

Shaken from his meditations, he lifted eyes and looked north. Not far from where he kneeled there stood a black hole in the fabric of the mountain. Lot stood and headed toward this mystery.

Rocky terrain and several curious ibex notwithstanding, he managed to reach his goal within a few minutes.

"Hmm, never saw this before," said he, standing in the mouth of a large cavern. No smell emanated from it, and because he felt led of the Spirit, he entered. Though dark from outside, light shimmered off cave walls inside, and Lot soon discovered the reason: a natural spring in its back section reflected sunlight from a large opening in the cavern ceiling.

Once he reached this spring, he bent and tasted of its waters.

Pure taste equaled its crystalline brilliance. A strange peace settled over the man as he there lingered in such a providential and unexpected abode. Sodom and all its corruption and rottenness seemed a world away. How could there even be evil men and cities in a land boasting such an oasis? Why even have cities? *The Lord provides for His own.* Did not Enoch say as much in his old writings?

When a wing of plovers settled at the cave mouth and began issuing their soft calls, Lot woke from his reverie and began the long trek home. On the way, he decided he would bring supplies and begin stocking the cave—for emergencies. If he could not find steady work, or Irith lost too much before they got her wagering under control, the family might be out of house and home. Would be nice to have a stocked cavern to turn to under such an event.

No one stopped him at Sodom's gate.

They seemed to have been waiting further in, near *Lagos* district where shrines to Diana vied for attention with temples of Dionysius and holy tabernacles.

No longer sanctuaries, these places now housed what Lot referred to as *Clergy Criminals.* He spotted a cabal lurking in the courtyard of Diana. In some ways they were worse than mindless mobs, for these were supposed elders and clerics and scribes and professionals.

Arrayed in fine robes and dyed cloaks (he wondered if he had colored some of them himself) seven men and two women in black veils descended upon Lot, circling him as he attempted to cross the courtyard. He had no weapon, except one.

He prayed to his Keeper, eyes remaining open and focused on those encroaching.

Two of the men carried stones, and Lot recognized them as those who had accosted him at the gates. A few wagged their tongues at him. He knew what that meant; some thugs here were just violent, wanting merely to harm. But others . . . many men in Sodom were of a different sort and sought to force themselves on anyone they could, be they women, men, or even children.

Like a glimmer of fire from Sheol, Lot saw a glint in the eyes of those men. The women would look on, simply watch.

It was not in Lot's nature to comprehend how women could condone acts of rape. Perhaps there were tragedies in their past which had turned their hearts of flesh into hearts of stone, seared their consciences as with a hot iron. He did not know. Could never understand such people.

How can I ever reach such lost souls? thought he just then, as they came on.

One braved a dart forward, and tugged on Lot's beard, an extreme insult.

Just as the others commenced with jeering and hysterics, a pair of well-heeled men stepped between them. These two were even better dressed, and boasted gemstones in their beards. They whistled and suddenly the aggressive group was flanked by urchins, all armed and looking as deranged as Hashnah had.

To Lot's surprise, the group dispersed with only a few muddled grunts and complaints.

"Thank you," he said to the pair of well-dressed men. "May the Lord's light shine—"

"They will seek you again," interrupted the younger one. Sunlight glinted off his necklace. "We could well be there for you hence, should you agree to our offer."

"Offer?"

This time the elder spoke, in a commanding arrogant tone. "We have upon many a time observed your fair daughters. In tabernacle. They are both of them lovely divine. We want their hands in marriage, you see. In exchange, we shall provide our continued protection." He leaned in as if revealing state secrets: "Know you half the city wants your blood? You surely must know. The other half seems to want your body. Without us, how long shall you survive, do you suppose?"

Turning to look upon the retreating backs of his oppressors, Lot gave serious consideration to this offer. They were right. He was well known, and more hated even than the tax collectors. "I must pray about it. Let me ask you, what family line hail you from? Have you a dowry worthy of women of God?"

They explained their descent from the line of Cush. Everyone knew Cushites were all excellent hunters, able combatants. But of course many claimed to be of the line of Cush, boasting how their many times great-grandfather was Nimrod himself.

A little ribbing and digging and Lot got another answer: they descended from Haran.

Which would make them distant cousins.

Each could afford a fine dowry. And they were well-spoken, mayhap they could even read. He promised to consider their offer and then begged their departure. A careful yet swift leg brought him home safely, where his daughters greeted him with hugs and queries after Joshua.

"He is well," replied Lot, removing his cloak before they could offer. "We made it out and to your uncle, and Abram has agreed to rear him." He chuckled. "The boy even hugged me. All is well on that field. Now, how fairs your mother?" For she had figured in his prayers upon the mount, and lay heavy on his mind the entire journey.

They lowered their voices, whispering that Irith had taken some water and a nit of wine, but would only take a few nibbles of wrapped raisin cakes.

"We think she does long to return to Shem's," conspired Ammi.

Lot had expected as much. This was not the first time Irith had fallen off the cart. In fact it happened almost every summer hiatus their first several years in Sodom, but she had resisted for the past two. Lot's hope that his wife had been cured of her longing for that heathen ritualized wagering now hung by a thread.

This, with his now daily waylays, conspired to make him consider two options: taking up the Haran men's offer, or leaving Sodom altogether. But that second would mean returning to Abram, like a whipped man who could not tend to his own family.

So instead—after ministering to his wife that afternoon—Lot took his daughters into the rear yard. As he fed their lamb, he explained the situation.

Following a long pause where both girls looked around in open-mouthed wonder, Charity looked at her father and asked, "What do *you* want us to do, father?"

Inwardly Lot sighed. He had no confidence in his ability to make decisions for himself, much less life decisions for his beloved girls. "This is a major choice, and no one can make it for you, no one should make it for you, but each one of you. Your happiness and wellbeing are more important to me than my safety."

Nervous smiles as they considered things again.

"What will happen if we say no?"

"Well, then we shall have to pack up and depend upon the mercy of my uncle again, or perhaps try to earn a living in neighboring Gomorrah."

Ammi, playing with her braid, settled down on the brickwork beside her father. "I know ye how much it shall hurt to go back to him. You shall feel . . . like as you have failed here. But you have not failed. Not us."

Charity came over, knelt before Lot and added: "Many fathers stroll this city. Some are abusive violent men. Others drunkards and philanderers. We would have none of them. You are a good father, the only one we would ever choose to have." She took his hands, and Lot noticed how soft hers were, despite the chores she daily performed. "We would not have our father feel as unto a failure. Tell us about these men, and if you think they will not hurt us, then we shall agree to wed them." Here she looked over at her younger sister, who nodded slowly, still that strange, blended expression of shy excitement on her face.

Trying not to cry for the beauty of his daughters—their hearts were as noble and selfless as that of their Great Aunt Sarai—Lot told of the well-groomed and well-spoken manner of the men.

When they at length agreed to the marriages, he bowed and fought tears.

"Uncle Abram was right," he voiced "you really are the greatest gifts from the Lord. You two and your mother." The sheep nuzzled his hand, demanding more food. "And you too, methinks!" Together all three laughed.

Just then Irith emerged from their house.

Apparently seeing them like that filled her with her own gladness of heart and, (supposed Lot) a sense of guilt for her actions.

He gestured her over and they all embraced.

That was the last moment of joy any of them would ever have in Sodom.

Within two weeks both girls were married, though certain factors kept them at home for the time, while their husbands took up residence nearby. Lot had made arrangements with them: they would have their paid thugs keep watch on him as he continued to sit in the gate. Their end— the receiving of his virgin daughters—seemed to him the better receipt, so he convinced them to wait a certain number of days before consummating the marriages, thus treating it more as a betrothal.

This gave his daughters time to acclimate to married life. (Both young women thanked their father for this needed delay, showering him with kisses on his cheeks.) During the day, they kept house at their respective husbands' abodes and engaged in home business activities there, mostly the spinning and trading of dyed wool, and in the evenings they returned home.

Lot was—for the time being—fairly well protected from Sodom's regular little mobs, but authorities now began to question him.

Their questioning soon developed into interrogations, followed by vicious attacks on his character, accusing him of lawlessness for speaking out against their new decrees. To flee seemed wise, as he grew overcome with feeling vanquished and small. Well he knew it would not be long ere he was arrested. As Sodomites rung him daily, mocking his efforts to turn them from their sinful ways, Lot reflected that his new sons-in-law must have powerful connections;

their thugs' presence a sign that a high price would be paid for beating or taking Lot away.

Indeed, he soon discovered that their group, which included a charter and paid membership, was called the *Young Leaders for Sodom's Tomorrow*.

Something about that title unsettled him.

Regardless of their intimidating presence, it was only a matter of time. Corruption ran deep, and lust for violence and hatred of dissention eventually overpower any fear of reprisal.

Everything changed on the last day of a week not long after the weddings. A bloodred sky gave bad tidings that morning, though Lot 's foreboding was briefly forgotten upon the ninth hour as he sat in the gates: two strange men dressed in the whitest garments he had ever beheld, entered Sodom.

Chapter Seven

On a bright summer day a few weeks following Lot's visit, Abraham (for so God did bestow this name upon him) sat in the open door of his tent. From here he watched his vast flocks and family community.

Of a sudden he looked across a field at a stand of terebinth trees, their leaves whispering in hot breeze. When he lifted his eyes, Abraham saw three men.

A stirring deep in his spirit. These were not mere men, but something . . . more.

Abraham ran from his tent to greet them, bowing low to the ground, saying "My Lord, if I have indeed found favor in Your sight, do not pass by Your servant. If You wait but a moment, and permit me, I shall bring water to wash Your feet. Please, rest Yourselves beneath this tree. I shall bring a morsel of bread, that You may refresh Your hearts. After that You may pass by, only see and let me show that You have come to Your servant."

As One, the three men said, 'Do as you have spoken.'

Like a faithful servant, Abraham and his family performed all his words.

Before taking their leave, the men gave a far greater gift to Abraham, promising not only another visit, but that upon visiting again, it would be when Sarai was giving birth.

To this the man of God could only bow and beam with greatest joy. He did not doubt his Lord's promise though he could not comprehend how it were possible, he being old and his wife long years past childbearing age. Indeed, upon the covenanted promise, he did hear Sarai's laughter from the other side of the tent flap behind him.

So also did the Lord hear it, and ask after it, as if doubt made no sense to He who had promised.

When the men turned eastward and began heading that way, distressing ruminations roused Abraham's spirit. He knew it must be of grave seriousness, for nothing but that could have dislodged his perfect joy.

He followed them.

Overheard them.

One of the men asked 'Shall I hide from Abraham what I am doing, since Abraham shall surely become a great and mighty nation, and all nations on earth shall be blessed in him? For I have known him, in order that he may command his children and his household after him, that they keep the way of the Lord, to do righteousness and justice, that the Lord may bring Abraham what He has spoken to him.'

Having heard this, and being both overwhelmed with honor and filled with foreboding (for they looked yonder toward Sodom as they spoke, and well did the man of God know how the cities down that way engaged in godless acts, even blasphemies and abominations), Abraham stood panting as the men turned to look on him.

Then spoke the Lord:

'The blood of innocents, as righteous Abel, cries out to Me, and because the outcry also of angels denouncing Sodom and Gomorrah is very great, I shall go down now and see whether they have done altogether according to these outcries against it that have come up to Me; and if not, I will know.'

Filling him with terror, Abraham watched as the men turned back toward Sodom, and stepped to head down that direction.

He ran and stood near unto his Lord. Though indeed he understood well that the Lord's righteous justice should be descending upon those wicked cities, he also understood that Lot and his family was down there. He blurted out "Would you also destroy the righteous with the wicked?"

The men paused in step.

Encouraged, Abraham continued, ignoring a rush of hot wind whipping his beard and pressing into his face: "Suppose there were fifty righteous within those cities; would You also destroy them and not spare them for the sake of those righteous that were in them? Far be it from You to do such a thing as this, to slay the righteous with the wicked; far be it from You!" His usual gruff voice was panicky, almost a shriek. "Shall not the Judge of all the earth do right?"

Abraham stood trembling, terrified the Lord would not respond at all, or simply show wisdom in His design, that was quite beyond the grasp of man, even one such as he.

Instead, the Lord said, 'If I find fifty righteous within Sodom, then I shall spare all the place for their sake.'

Well did this prince of men know that the Lord would not find so many righteous within Sodom's gates. In fact, he could not name even a dozen. So he, braving the Lord's grace and patience, humbled himself yet boldly asked if the Lord would spare the cities for forty-five righteous. Finding the Lord willing in this, he asked after forty righteous? Again, mercy

121

promised on all for the sake of the few.

Heartened, Abraham asked the same of thirty righteous, then twenty. Finally he asked if the Lord would spare the city for the sake of ten righteous men.

By now Abraham was sweating and exhausted from trembling.

But he had his promise in hand: the Lord vowed to spare Sodom if ten righteous were found within her gates.

It was still no guarantee the city would be spared, Abraham reflected as he watched the men descend in the direction that would lead to Sodom. Were there even ten good men there?

He knew of only one.

As he returned to his tents, Abraham wiped his face dry and sought to shake off his fright and concern, for Sarai knew nothing of all this. She would be rejoicing, for in His greatness the Lord had promised them a trueborn son.

Tonight I shall give thanks in prayer—and beseech the Lord's protection on Lot and his family.

Chapter Eight

A mighty western wind rushed through Sodom, bringing with it the stink of her putrescent valley of bones out there.

Lot knew for a fact some of that odor came from the rotting corpses of newborn babes. It struck him as particularly wicked. Now as he walked the streets toward Sodom's gate, hearing babies cry and adults shout (and oft even adults crying), Lot was struck by a different thought: how do they choose who lives past birth? Who are they to make such decisions?

Like a high noon shadow, a gaggle of *Young Leaders of Sodom's Tomorrow* trailed him.

They were getting restless, he knew. Their own leaders had their prize—Lot's daughters—but the 'gems had not yet been set', as the saying went.

If he was not careful, it would not be long before his protectors deformed into his enemies.

Even now they did little to deter would-be attacks. At a mead and wine vendor Lot was jostled. A large man resembling Ham uttered a sarcastic apology: "Oh, sorry little judge, I saw you not." A whiff of imbibed mead at his passing.

When at last Lot reached the gate he took up his usual spot, by now festooned with trash and defiled with the stains and reek of urine.

Still, he carried Enoch's papyrus and began condemning these Sodomites for their disregard of the Lord's design. As usual, a crowd soon formed. A mob. The *Young Leaders of Sodom's Tomorrow* encircled him, but this human barricade had many cracks in it.

Hissing and spitting commenced, joined with cussing. Most reached through gaps between Young Leaders. Lot continued bringing forth the truth. Spittle soaked his cloak.

Not a single bubble did he wipe off.

On pausing to catch his breath, he looked up. Strange crimson clouds whirled overhead, occasionally rumbling in unusual crackles and booms.

Briefly he thought he saw fire swirling amid those eerie clouds.

As he resumed recitation, dusk began to fall.

Then came Lot to the section where Enoch pronounces the Lord's design for marriage and intimate relations: '*So God created man in His own image, in the image of God created He him; male and female created He them.*'

This seemed to rile the mob, for several men there on that strange morning were dressed in the style of women, even with veils, embracing a current vogue of male Sodomites acting as females and dishonoring both sexes in the process.

'*And the Lord saw that it was not good for man to be alone, so He created woman and gave her to the man, for the Lord has ordained that a man should leave his father and mother and be joined to his wife, a woman.'*

Suddenly the mob—which included a number of women—set upon the *Young Leaders*.

Lots protectors fought back.

But he could tell their hearts were not in it; some of them had given dirty looks at his reciting of *Enoch*. He set the tablet down and, feeling the old fearful trembling commence, decided it was time to flee homeward.

Just then as he stood, two startling events silenced everyone.

The heavens exploded overhead with the loudest thunderclap Lot (and likely everyone else, judging by their startled motions) had ever heard, just as two striking men dressed in fine pristine white linen garments entered Sodom through its western gate.

As everyone stood in shock at these two events, Lot pushed his way forward, approaching these two well-dressed men.

127

For he sensed in his spirit these men were sent of God—as Abram had once explained to him of a similar encounter. He bowed. "Behold now, my lords, turn I pray you into your servants' house, and spend the evening there. I shall wash your feet, and when you rise up early you may go your way. Only please, spend the evening in the safety of my abode."

But the men declined. 'Nay, we shall abide in the city square tonight.'

An odd light in their unblinking eyes. Like looking into a star, Lot mused. Though fascinated by this, he was troubled by their intention to remain in Sodom's square. They would undoubtedly be accosted, molested, or attacked in some way.

Even now Sodom's men—including those dressed as women—gazed hungrily at these two appealing beings sent of God.

So Lot pressed vehemently, insisting they come with him and spend the evening beneath the safety of his roof. At last they agreed. With apparent reluctance, the *Young Leaders of Sodom's Tomorrow* guarded Lot and his two guests all the way home. As they trod rough streets, Lot heard the mob whispering and conniving beyond them.

It would be a very long night.

To his relief, Irith was up and about tending to house and engaged in their side employment. Because it was already evening, his daughters were home as well, along with Ammi's husband who stood speaking to her in what Lot considered rather aggressive tones. When the man discovered Lot was home, however, he took his leave, slowing on his way to the door when he observed his father-in-law's two striking guests.

Once Lot had introduced them to his family, he set about doing just as he promised, washing the men's feet and baking unleavened bread and feasting as best they could considering the hard times.

Amid this cozy intimate feast, two developments sowed dread into Lot and the women. One was celestial, the other very much human.

Thunderclaps and odd rumblings accompanied intermittent flashes, as if great fires were being lit and then swiftly doused overhead. Just outside their abode, angry Sodomites gathered, the men of Sodom young and old. Sitting at their small rough-planed almug table, the family heard this mob utter invectives as each arriving member roiled each other up.

At length it seemed every man in town milled and broiled outside their home.

Wooden braces were placed before doors, and Lot and Irith closed all the shutters. As he was closing the last pair, he observed that instead of pitch darkness, or hazy moonlight, an unnerving red glow illumined everything, even impinging on shadows with its flickering red glare.

They tried to lay down to sleep, hoping the mob would grow weary and disperse.

Presently voices began calling for Lot.

Shaking, he rose. His two guests of honor stood nearby the door, as if awaiting him. Angry voices beckoned just beyond that solid wood barrier.

"Where are those lookers which came into thy house this night? Bring them out that we may lie with them!"

This his great fear, Lot stood momentarily stricken in place.

Shaking his head though he removed the brace and went out the door unto them and shut it after him, not willing that these Sodomites should have even one more glance of his revered guests. "I beg you, my brethren, do not do this wicked thing. They are not like you, but from afar, and they are innocent of your ways."

Back inside, he considered his options how he might possibly conciliate here.

131

Critical it was to give the *appearance* that he wanted to appease them. That he was willing to satisfy their desires with an offering. He knew many of those men outside his house who stood in that sinister slanting red light; they were members of the politico, of the church, whose sexual appetites were so far from the Lord's design, that many no longer even looked upon women.

So he decided *that* might be the way to appease them.

"But look, I have two daughters, and neither have ever been with a man; let me, I beg you, bring them out unto you, and you may do as you see fit with them, only lay not a hand upon my revered guests. They have come under the shadow of my roof, and I will see no harm done to them."

From behind the door, Lot heard gasps. His wife and daughters, God bless their innocent souls, must not have understood what he knew:

that such godless men as these out here would have nothing to do with his virgin daughters.

If his guests were indeed sent from God as he suspected they were, then surely it was his duty as the Lord's servant to protect them—at all costs.

Not completely unexpected, the mob disregarded his offer.

"Please, do not do this evil in seeking to lay with my guests!"

"Evil?" screamed several men. "Who are you to call our ways evil? If we love to do something, then it is good. Is it not love to bestow our pleasures or to take pleasure in another? Let all men do as they love, for that is love! And you—some wretched foreigner, who thinks he is royalty as kin of Abram—dare you tell us how to live?"

Lot's head and spirits drooped as they renewed their attacks on his person.

"Move aside! Let us in." Others declared: "You hear this one? This sojourner, this foreigner, come into our city and sits as judge over us?" Another added his voice in vehement tones: "You ought not to have intervened. We saw these men and claimed right of them as ours. Now you have stepped between us and our claim; it shall be the worse for you now!"

Even as the heavens rumbled and blared overhead, these venomous creatures mobbed Lot, so that he was pressed against his own door.

Face pushed against rough-hewn wood. Arms slammed painfully between the door and his aggressors. Suddenly the pressure vanished, and he felt strong hands pulling him back inside. While one stood him firmly, the other slammed and barred Lot's door.

Even as Lot watched and tried to catch his breath, his two guests raised their hands, palms facing toward the door: brilliant white light burst forth, somehow passing through the door and walls and momentarily vanquishing the sickly crimson glow outside.

Both men then lowered their hands.

Scrambling along with his astonished family, Lot moved to the window and flung wide the shutters.

To their utter confusion, every man out there was now stumbling around. Many rubbed their eyes. Others staggered like drunken men, bumping into each other. It was as if they had all— "Are they blinded?" Charity gasped.

Silence from the stoic men in those garments white as snow.

In time, as the family listened to heavenly rumblings, those blind men stumbling around slowly dispersed (using their hands and shouts to move about), apparently wearied from searching for Lot's door.

When all was quiet save for thundering and strange explosions overhead, Ammi asked "Are we safe now?"

The men shook their heads and turned to Lot.

By now it was nearly morning. Something in the air summoned tiny cracklings of lightning through their hair—everyone's but the two men who had blinded Lot's enemies.

On that morning before dawn, when the air and light and even the sound of their voices were all curious departures from anything they had known, Lot and his family turned to their guests in wonderment.

Waiting.

"Surely did the Lord Almighty send you to us for such an hour as this," Lot whispered.

Their divine faces now shown signs of concern. One of the men laid a hand firmly on Lot's right shoulder. 'Have you any other kin here in this city? Sons-in-law, perhaps? More daughters or sons?'

In the same hasty manner, the other man said, 'If you do, run hence and summon them. Take all you wish not to lose, for you must flee this place.'

Irith took Lot's hand. His daughters gathered near, like small birds.

Now the other man spoke: 'We will destroy this place, and those cities around it, for the cry of them is waxen great before the face of the Lord; and the Lord Himself has indeed sent us for this purpose.'

"Father?" Ammi murmured. She sounded like unto a child.

Lot hastened next door, observing on the way that no one remained of his pursuers. He also observed that deviant glow cast down upon Sodom by angry heavens.

His sons-in-law were speaking among themselves in their house. They seemed undisturbed by recent events, neither upset by the mob that was nor concerned with the light which now discolored even their walls and flesh. "Up! Make haste and get you out of this place, for the Lord is about to destroy Sodom, and Gomorrah too!"

137

Both men looked at him for a moment, and then at each other, whereupon they burst out laughing.

Though Lot made another attempt, they remained unmoved.

He left them. Of greater concern was his family, blood of his blood.

Overhead, yellow and pink light seemed to vie for predominance with those red roiling clouds. In his own house, Lot found his daughters toting pelt bags bursting with articles of their clothing. Irith paced. Gazing at everything with peculiar longing eyes.

'You must hurry,' urged the men to Lot. 'The appointed time is upon you. Arise, take your wife and two daughters, lest they be consumed in the iniquity of the city!'

Too shaken to reply, filled with regret for his failures to save these wicked Sodomites—even his own sons-in-law—Lot lingered in the entranceway.

This was too much for his divine protectors. They grabbed hold of Lot's and Irith's hands, pushing them out the door before taking the hands of his daughters as well and taking them out of the house. As Lot would realize, they did this because the Lord was being merciful.

With great haste they did lead these terrified people of God out of Sodom.

It was in the sandy plains just outside those old familiar gates, as they were passing a great carved sphinx, that they raised their voices (for the heavens did bellow and erupt with flame, and the first fiery stones burst out from those angry clouds to scythe into Sodom's buildings).

Booming louder than human voices, and echoing across the plain, they spoke:

FLEE FOR YOUR LIVES!

LOOK NOT BEHIND THEE, NEITHER STAY THOU IN ALL THIS PLAIN

ESCAPE TO THE MOUNTAIN, LEST THOU BE
CONSUMED!

Shaking with fright, Lot yelled back in despair
"Oh Lord, let it not be!"

Appearing like a mirage to their left, that
same tiny village Lot had passed on his way home
now caught his eye. A thought struck him at its
sight. He called to his rescuers: "Behold now, I
have found grace in your eyes, for you have saved
my life and delivered my family from destruction.
You have magnified God's grace in the eyes of His
people! Yet I cannot escape to the mountain, it is
too far, and for certain some disaster shall strike
us if we seek to reach it." He paused to catch his
breath, and because he saw that his rescuers were
slowing down with clear designs to return to the
city.

"Behold now this village nearby, and see it is
very small, one which could not have participated
in the sins of Sodom and Gomorrah. Oh let us

escape hither—is it not a simple innocent hamlet?—and our souls shall live."

I ACCEPT THIS ALSO, said the men, their eyes like fire and their tunics too bright to look long upon.

TURN INTO THIS VILLAGE THITHER IF YOU SO LIKE. ONLY, KEEP FLEEING AND TURN NOT BACK TO THOSE CITIES OF SIN.

So Lot and his family turned in toward the village, which would be called Zoar.

But as they entered that place, the heavens opened and fire and brimstone fell with furious rage upon Sodom and Gomorrah, and also upon Zeboiim and Admah further north along the Sea.

Chapter Nine

They were only a few whiskers inside of Zoar when Lot noticed their deliverers had vanished.

All thought narrowed down to sharp focus upon getting his family safely to the northernmost section of this settlement. Hoping as he ran that there might be a stone structure there. Not likely, considering the size of this village.

"Run!" he shouted to Irith and the girls ahead of him, waving them forward though they had slowed not a bit.

Lot knew they must be feeling what he was feeling. Furnace heat licking at their heels, and all while colossal booms and incessant ground-trembling, ear-splitting hammerings continued unabated behind them. Beneath all this celestial clatter, barely registering yet still horrifically there, were screams. Death-cries of tens of thousands of people.

Of sinners, unrepentant and unredeemed.

Oh, how that man knew horror for them, for well he knew where their eternal souls were destined when done they were in moments with their mortal bodies.

At a sudden burst of flame so bright it briefly cast away the few remaining shadows among small brick abodes, Irith stopped and stood motionless, panting. Lot heard her weeping.

"We left our bronze coins," she shrieked over the carnage. "I kept also a few minas of silver in the—" She spun around, to turn back for their money.

Lot was about to catch her up and turn her back the right direction, but as he ran up to his wife, Irith's eyes suddenly widened and appeared to solidify. Then as a cry emerged from her mouth, it was abruptly cut off. Her entire body transformed, flesh and even clothing becoming like unto a great pillar of salt. With the blistering wind blowing, her tunic hardened as it billowed out, pausing that way like water frozen in a flash.

Despite his utter shock and terror and immediate sense of mad loss, Lot had the presence of mind to warn his girls against the same transgression: when they heard their mother's scream over the rumblings and crashes of this violent unprecedented storm, they began to turn.

He yelled "Do not look back! Keep you moving forward. Heed me in this or we die!"

Lot could not linger; heat was causing him to break out in horrific sweat, and it sounded as if the fiery darts from heaven were nearing them. He had also begun to hack on acrid fumes.

In moments he caught up with his daughters and, wrapping an arm around each, led them on, pushing and even at times holding them up and keeping them from stumbling over the village's rough lane.

Not many villagers were around, but those who were did the same.

Soon a small crowd mirrored Lot and his daughters, while others remained outside their abodes to stand and watch the destruction open-mouthed.

At last they reached the northernmost point, and here Lot shoved Ammi and Charity into the darkness of a small brick abode, heedless of its owners.

In fact, no one else seemed to be inside.

Huddling around him, the girls wept and trembled. It did not take long for them to realize who was missing.

"Mother?" Charity cried.

"Where is she?" Ammi scrambled back toward the doorway.

Lot snatched her arm and yanked her back down. Though it broke his heart to say it, he told them she was lost.

The raging fiery storm continued outside their small hiding place unabated for a long terrifying stretch. Seeking to be strong for his girls, who had lost not only their mother but their entire way of life and everything they had ever known, Lot alternated between embracing them and offering encouraging words. He was forced to raise his voice, but with the tempest it only came out as whispers.

Hours passed in this stricken state. Fear and grief inside, rumbling and quaking and distant screams outside.

Sometime late that evening—judging by the darkness (or perhaps smoke palls covering the sun) mitigated by flickering glow of firelight—the terrifying sounds of destruction at last died down.

In this numbing silence Lot stood and crept toward the door. With his hand on its warm wooden planks, he whispered, "Stay here a moment, girls." Immediately upon opening the door he was assaulted by a stench as unto eggs let go too long. Covering his mouth and nose with a parcel of blue-dyed cloth, he stepped outside, easing the door closed behind.

Though it was full dark—no stars—he could see his way around quite well.

Well enough to observe villagers staggering about, clearing fallen goods, righting overturned carts, and rounding up their beasts who had been stirred nigh unto madness by the monstrous storm.

The further south he trod in this small hamlet the worse this situation became. Soon he spotted fresh corpses lying prostrate hither and yawn. Faces all a peculiar cerulean shade.

Those which were not scorched black, anyway.

A tickle in his throat; Lot hacked and spat.

When it at last subsided, he found himself standing directly before his wife. Or rather, the motionless pillar into which his wife had been cursed. Slowly did he circle around until he faced her. Yes, this was Irith. How white her flesh had become, nothing like the dark olive tone he had always loved and admired. But those were her hands, outstretched as in the day she came running up to greet him upon their betrothal.

Gingerly he reached out a hand to touch her brackish one. But at the faintest touch he realized his wife was well and truly gone; this was only some kind of salt, a mere lifeless pillar.

And where was her eternal soul? Where had it flown to when her body was cursed so?

For a moment, no longer, he wept.

But it was hard to breathe here under the stench of this poisonous air and the stink of fallen villagers, who seemed to have soiled themselves in their efforts.

Afresh with terror Lot now backtracked, cloth still over his mouth and nose, little good though it did. Avoiding those few remaining on their feet, Lot sped back to his daughters. Despite the fug in the air from smoke, he managed to find their borrowed abode, and he burst inside and slammed the door behind.

Startled as they were, his girls relaxed a bit on seeing who it was standing there.

"Papa? What is it? What is going on out there?" Charity asked, cradling a crying Ammi upon her bosom. "We thought we heard a pig squealing and someone falling over—"

"Get up with you," he ordered. "Quickly now, we must flee this place."

Though they still looked shaken, Lot's daughters did not question him.

At the door he told them to keep their eyes down, and hold a section of their tunics over their mouths. And when he opened the door, he knew this was wise advice. Something in the air was not simply foul, but lethal.

Few villagers remained on their feet.

Of those still alive, most were hacking and guzzling what water they found to soothe that tickle in their throats. Lot very much doubted the water here would help.

Likely it too was poisoned.

Fires big and small lent all the light they needed. He was careful to avoid looking back toward Sodom, a city divinely judged, and made sure to keep the girls before him to ensure they too would keep their eyes focused ahead. *Only* forward. Not back.

It took not but a hundred paces to leave that village and enter the last stretch of plain before encountering a stand of terebinth trees at the foothills of Mount Sodom. Even these trees seemed to be dying, all discolored and sad.

As they fled, Lot reflected on that tiny village. Perhaps it was as the angels (for he now had no doubts they were such) had said, and because of God's mercy on Lot, they would spare it. Certainly it had not suffered the brunt of burning stone and fiery rain. Mayhap its survivors would even take lesson from the heavenly doom they had just witnessed in judgment against its bigger sister cities, and its people repent of any sins and be saved.

He hoped so.

He hoped their waters would not remain foul for too long.

Yet even as he pushed his daughters ahead toward the Mount, Lot felt the weight of his failures. Only hoping that the Lord's using him to save Joshua and Zoar and his daughters, and His clear desire and efforts to preserve Lot, displayed divine forgiveness and great mercy for any failures real or imagined.

Despite their grief and frayed emotions, their pretty faces covered with dust and lineated by tear-trails, Charity and Ammi complained of fatigue and weakness.

They were then at the foot of Mount Sodom and beginning to climb. It did Lot's heart good to hear them reacting in such a normal way, their whining voices and slow-moving bodies. He urged them on, upwards, hundreds of feet until at last they reached a path he remembered.

Up here they found clean air, untainted by stench or heat.

For the first time he dared to look back toward their hometown.

Darkness broken by sporadic fires, made the sight stunning, as horrific an evil display as ever he had witnessed. No buildings remained. All had been pulverized and burned to ash. No signs of life, human or animal. Not even a single tree or shrub had survived.

"An entire civilization wiped out in the twinkling of an eye," he whispered in awe.

To either side of him, Lot's daughters stood on unsteady legs. Observing his liveliness, they too turned to look. Both girls gasped.

"That," pointed Lot, "is what happens when an entire civilization forsakes the Lord, disregards His will and design for them, indulges in abominations, and uses edicts to force all and sundry to partake of their iniquities with them."

As they would at a family member's funeral, all three stood in sullen silence for a long stretch. Lot then cried out in heaves of lamentation, rent his clothes to the waist and wailed for the lost. So as not to offend the Great Judge, he did this not for those cities and fallen sinners down there, but for his wife. When he had finished, he fell silent.

No one moved or spoke for a time.

Tranquility broke when a bird sounded from nearby. It was a dove. Lot silently thanked the Lord for that. It somehow seemed appropriate.

Now did he lead his girls slowly, for they were all as weary as ever they had been.

So quiet up here upon the mount you could almost hear angel voices—or so it seemed to Ammi: "I do believe I heard them just now. Weeping even!"

To a man of God like Lot, such an idea seemed verging on blasphemy, that angels would ever weep, those living flames who always do stand in the presence of the Holy One. But he did not correct her.

They were broken. Traumatized. Young women who had just lost their mother and home—*and husbands*, he now remembered. He did not mourn those two men, who had used him.

He thanked God that his daughters had not given their most precious gifts to those heathen Sodomites.

At the cave mouth they drew back.

Comforting them with gentle murmurs of reassurance, that he knew this cave and it was safe, the young women let him guide them inside. Using flint and twigs he prepared a fire. It set them on edge at first; perhaps the sight of flames would always summon their worst memories. But its warmth soon beckoned.

Gathered together in a huddle around a controlled campfire, the shattered family ate and did not speak. Occasionally someone coughed. Even those fits soon calmed. Sleep came hard.

As they tried to shake off their many recent traumas, Charity glanced around the cave.

Lot was aware, but too exhausted to recognize what it was her gaze fell upon, over there in the corner, its bottom half not quite concealed by pelt coverings.

It was the boiled wine he had stowed here. In case water proved scarce.

He never touched the stuff himself. Probably a few sips would suffice to bring on deep sleep, and help him forget his sufferings—for a time.

But Charity knew about boiled wine.

Her husband had oft partaken of it when she visited him. She knew its potency.

Chapter Ten

Abraham rose early the following morning.

He returned to that promontory where he had formerly stood before the Lord, and lo, smoke from the down country still billowed up as fumes from a great furnace.

In his grief (for so Abraham knew there had not been even 10 righteous men down in those wicked cities of the plain, but he trusted the Lord had delivered Lot and his family from it, and deigned not to humiliate Lot by seeking him, as if to rescue him back from his follies), he fled that land and headed toward the south country.

Between Kadesh and Shur did Abraham dwell, and he sojourned in Gerar.

During these days, his wife Sarai waxed round and did glow with the life of their promised child within her womb. In due time, according to the word of the Lord, Sarai gave birth to a son of promise. And they named him Isaac.

The seed of all God's chosen people had been delivered into the world according to a covenant made on the eve of destruction, for the Lord is faithful.

Faithful even unto His promises of wrath for unrepentance.

Never did Abraham see his nephew Lot again. Yet in his later years of gladness he did hear of him, that Lot had survived and a new people did come from his own seed.

Yet the strange manner of their conception did not reach this Mighty Prince's ears.

Chapter Eleven

At that time and in those days Lot and his daughters lived in a state of constant uncertainty and inward disquiet.

Most every spot, cliff, and promontory from that side of Mount Sodom showed only complete annihilation of every city in the plains near the Jordan: Sodom, Gomorrah, along with Zoboiim and Admah, westward of those sister cities. By the end of that first week, all fires had died down. In their absence, the plains of the Jordan had become plains again, uninterrupted by any cityscape.

Not a single building remained. No trees or streets. Not even a scrub bush to mark where civilization had flourished—if in the most abominable of manners.

Lot had last taken a gander three days before the Sabbath. He knew then that once the autumn winds blew in, those scorched patches would be coated in dust and dirt and leaves, and by this time next year it would be as if those cities had never existed.

He no longer took in the vistas.

Instead, Lot remained in their cave, cleaning out critter leavings and sweeping every corner and parcel of floor clean. He did not trim his beard, only his hair.

"Why do the walls sparkle when the sun looks in from above, Papa?" even Charity had reverted to calling him 'Papa' in place of the more mature *Father*.

He feared what this indicated: that because of their traumas, even his eldest daughter had regressed in her mind to the days of her girlhood. Using endearing terms. Following him around. Indeed, since arriving here both daughters had slept close by his own pallet, until Lot told them they must sleep further apart, and he took a smaller chamber deeper within the cave as his own bedroom.

"They shine so," replied Lot while filling a sheep's bladder with water from the spring, "because they are made of salt. Much of this mount is comprised of salt rock. It catches and throws sunlight. In days past, miners from Gomorrah would harvest the salt here. But . . . they developed other desires and busied themselves with other occupations."

Each day in late afternoon, the man did wander out to hunt their food.

He carried an adze he had purchased last year from a worker of bronze in Zeboiim, and a small dagger. With these he could scrounge up an ibex if he were careful to sneak upon one in its sleep. They made for tough but hearty meals. Mostly though Lot spent these hours before dusk just walking and praying. How to find his way back to faith, to believing. Oh, believed he still in the greatness of his heavenly Father—for of a certainty he did fear God as much and more than ever. Yet to believe now for the Lord's blessings . . .

It was a struggle for which he had no wisdom to tackle.

If only Abram were here. He would know what to say to help me, to show me how to help my daughters.

Daily he saw them losing hope and joy, even as he sought to restore them.

They said they could no longer see anyone moving around down in Zoar.

Often morning mist and daily rain prohibited their sight of it, yet no sounds of life reached their ears. To Lot as to his daughters, it seemed all the world had been destroyed in the fire from the sky.

Many a time did Lot ponder leaving this infernal mount. But he feared what they might see. Did all cities on earth now look as unto Sodom? Destroyed and swallowed up?

In all his wanderings and wonderings and prayers, the man did not imagine nor did it come into his heart to consider his present duty if they were truly the last people on earth. Yet what the man did not think of, the woman did, for Charity felt as many a woman felt in those days: a duty to continue the family line.

Only, so far as she knew, there was only one man left to provide seed for her family line.

Chapter Twelve

By the end of their second month up in Mount Sodom, Charity and Ammi knew something had to be done, for their father had grown distant and low.

He did still provide for them, food and clothing. To their wonder he had even stocked the cave with dyes and tin basins to color small articles of clothing, their linens and half-tunics and mantles. Yet even when he worked this special skill, Lot no longer sang to the Lord as in days of old.

Far more worrying to Charity, however, was how old he now appeared.

If it was as they feared, that all the world of men had been destroyed as in the days of Noah (for so their father had told them from that writing of Enoch who did walk with God), then it was up to them to obey the oldest command of all, the very first directive of God to humankind: Be fruitful and multiply!

Whenever she was not sewing or preparing meal or any of their dozen daily chores, or encouraging her little sister, Charity found herself watching their father.

Observing him . . . viewing with different eyes.

If only Mama were here. Life would be simpler, though she had not been so young either. Past the age of childbearing, mayhap. Perhaps Charity would have been brought to this unforeseen state regardless.

Mournful winds whistled through their strange home.

Inside the cave towards its back, a gaping fissure, almost circular, shimmered daily. Through this column fresh air spiraled, causing whistles while taking with it any odors which would have accumulated. *It truly is a fine place, so far as cave dwelling goes*, she mused.

Could it be a place to renew mankind?

None of them were yet ready to leave, though Ammi asked just now (as often she did) if they could go down to inspect Zoar. "Perhaps there are survivors," she said almost desperately.

"Not until Papa says it is safe," Charity replied with exasperation. She set her half-sewn dress down and stood to stretch. "You know he says the air is evil down there."

A cough turned their attention toward the mouth of the cave. Since his venture through Zoar, Lot had suffered a lingering hacking cough. Together they helped him haul his catch of the day, a stripling ibex with long jagged horns.

While they dragged it inside and Lot took a swig of water, Charity watched him.

"Papa," said she with a soft hand upon his elbow, "why not take you a bath down in the spring? Perhaps you might rub some cassia oil on afterward, to cleanse thyself and to ward off odors," trying not to sound like she found his smell offensive. She did not. Rather, Charity had other reasons for this suggestion.

Looking back at her, he nodded, even managing a forced smile. "Yes. Say you I stinketh?"

Ammi covered a giggle—the first since their flight from Sodom.

Charity grinned. "No. Only that I do believe you would feel refreshed."

While their father bathed down at the glistening spring, Charity took her little sister aside. Cleaning their father's pallet—fresh raven feathers for his pillow, clean linen washed in goat's tallow and alkali—she explained her plan.

"I know you want not to believe it, but it seems likely we are the last people."

Ammi groaned, nearly dropping a pillow. "I will not accept that as truth! Surely the Lord would spare others as He spared us!"

Quick now did Charity check outside this chamber. No, Lot had not heard and was not coming their way. "Keep thy voice down. Yes, I hope that others are out there too, somewhere. Yet even if they are, we are the last of *our* family:

you, me, and Papa. Father Abram was dwelling not far when the heavens reigned down that terrible fire; surely he and Aunt Sarai and all our line are gone. We must ensure that our family line—if not mankind itself—endures." She observed how uncomfortable Ammi was becoming, squirming and busying herself without looking upon her sisters' face. Had Ammi too considered their uncommon and desperate situation, to stumble upon similar uncomfortable lines of thought?

She continued, knowing her next words would forever alter their lives. "Remember you the Lord's first command to Father Adam and to Mother Eve, as Papa read us from Enoch's tablet?"

Ammi paused in her ministrations. Visibly trembling now, she stood and quoted without looking Charity in the eye: "Be fruitful and multiply. Fill the earth." Soon as she had said these words, Ammi ran around the bed to Charity, who stood a hand taller.

"Oh, tell me not thou art considering what I fear most?"

With a soft hand Charity gently cupped her sister's chin, pulling it up to look into her eyes. "Tonight I shall lie with Papa. He will come into me and give me his seed, and we shall continue our family line—if not the race of men."

Ammi closed her eyes and bowed as Charity released her.

"Oh heavens above! Sheol beneath! This must of a surety be sin, for sure I am that I did hear that Sodomites performed such acts."

Charity was quick to correct her, saying, "Yes indeed, I am sure some did, but out of lust and desire. I do this . . . I *must* do this, out of necessity, out of obedience to our Lord and Creator."

Not yet did Charity tell her the hardest part. She would save that, until Ammi was convinced of the need, of their absolute duty to perform such a task.

Shaking her head, tears promising to fall at the corners of her eyes, her little sister said, "It matters not, anyhow, as Papa would never do such a thing. No. He would rather all mankind die out than do such wickedness."

"He shall not know, neither shall he find out."

They finished the pallet just as another gust blizzarded through, ruffling fresh linens and tossing their hair all about. Autumn was fast approaching. Firewood needed gathering and stone fences needed building, to keep warm and protected from wildlife as they settled in for a long winter. How nice it would be to be expecting a blessing, during those chill and sure-to-be difficult dark days.

Throwing her arms up as her hair settled, Ammi exclaimed, "How could he not know?"

With a gesture, Charity led her out to the large cavern area, where she hauled up that large old clay jar of wine. "Papa never touches this stuff, and Bazeus once told me tale on how those who never partake of the vine, are those most sensitive and effected by it."

She now took a deep breath to steady her nerves to share her plan.

"We shall serve Papa tonight, ply him with generous amounts of this wine, until he knows not what is happening or who he is with. Then . . . then I shall go in and lie down beside him." She did not say the rest. Could not. Was she for a truth considering this? Would her plan even work? Could anything make a father not recognize his own daughter? Indeed, her 'husband' Bazeus had told her many tales of drunkards, and how they often forgot an evening's carousing upon new morning's light.

In the hallowed silence which followed, they listened only to murmuring wind, which did carry upon its back a pleasant scent of cardamom and terebinth. At length, Ammi suggested something Charity had also wondered: "Is this some kind of punishment, that we must do this thing? This a . . . oh, I know not. Is it the Lord's way of chastising us for not being better examples to our neighbors? Poor old Ebenezer and Maria, and their dogs, and our little lamb. All burnt up and gone. Think you if we had been better servants of the Lord, you would not now have to—"

She could not even say it.

Charity interrupted her besides, telling her the very thing she most feared to speak.

"You must lay down with him too, on the morrow's evening." At this pronouncement she turned from looking upon her little sister's face.

For a long span she spoke not a word, until at last Ammi opened her mouth and, crying, asked in a small girlish voice, "But why? Please, please do not make me—"

"What if my womb is closed like Aunt Sarai's?" it was a true and deep fear of most women in those days. A common suffering, a closed womb. "We must

171

ensure that our line—if not the line of all mankind—endures beyond we three. So yes, you must do your part as well. I shall go first, tonight. Tomorrow you—"

"But I have never known a man." Ammi bowed once again, her long dark hair hanging and flowing in breeze. "I never lay with Gerar. Mother never even told me how!"

Being a couple years older, Charity had the benefit of this knowledge, their mother having spoken with her of it upon her betrothal. She could not be sure why Irith had not done so with Ammi. Perhaps their father's deal with the men, to wait, had prompted Irith to postpone the sharing of such knowledge, so as to spare her youngest child and keep her as the virginal apple of her eye as long as possible.

Whatever the case, Charity felt it her responsibility to do this; and with what she had been told, and the experience she would have tonight, she felt confident there would be sufficient knowledge to share with Ammi.

Hopefully it would prepare her as best as possible.

Anon evening arrived.

The women had prepared a hearty feast of ibex ribs and pearlized onions (harvested on a plateau not far from their cave), with boiled chickpeas and salt. At first when Charity offered her father some wine, he refused. Yet with persistence and the argument that he needed it for his stomach's infirmity, and to help forget—if only for a night—'our great sorrow and loss', she managed to get him to sip wine.

Each subsequent sip and quaff proved considerably easier.

Soon Lot began to smile. On the pouring of a fresh cup, he began even to sing, breaking out into an old chaunt handed down from his father Haran, and his father Terah and on back supposedly to Noah himself.

Or so the men of the family always claimed.

His unfortunate voice breaking on higher notes made Ammi giggle.

Charity watched her closely. 'Twas clear her dear little sister was looking with different eyes upon their father, just as she, Charity, had been doing of late.

Not as 'Papa', but as a man.

One who could and perhaps even should, supply seed for their family.

It was full dark out. With Charity's aid, Lot rose and staggered at last to his chamber. He fell onto his pallet and mumbled something; she caught words to suggest he were speaking to Irith. At the jagged fissure which served as doorway, she observed him for a time. At length he began to snore quietly.

She found Ammi sitting still upon her downy pillow at the meal.

Crickets chirped outside the cavemouth several dozen yards away, beyond their makeshift gate of logs and stones.

"Are you going to do it?" Ammi did not look up, but only gazed into the fire.

Charity bit her lip. "Yes. It must be done." She imbibed here quickly a cup of that wine, until her head swam with its power. She did turn then but reconsidered something before facing her sister. "Pray for me." Then she left Ammi and headed toward their fathers' chamber, deeper inside their cavern. If asked, she could not then or later have said if she sought prayer for a healthy womb and fertile seed . . . or for forgiveness from the Lord.

At the fissure she waited a moment.

Lot snored, tossed.

Beginning to tremble yet also feeling emboldened by the wine, Charity inhaled deep and slow. Her heart now beat ever so much as it had done on that terrible day when they fled Sodom.

After removing her sandals, she did then slip out of her underclothes. In silence they fell to stony cavern floor like flax, though the woman felt the weight of their loss should have sounded loud, and rung strange tidings throughout that cave. Glad at least for the darkness, Charity padded over to her father and lay down upon his pallet.

He slept only in a linen shift, twisted and unbound from his tossing.

Closing her eyes now, Charity whispered "Lot?" It was the first time she ever spoke her father's name to him. Fear kept her from calling him 'father' or 'papa' now.

Lot turned over, muttered "Irith?" and lay still again.

That was as Charity had hoped. She began to do what her mother had explained to her, except that her mother had meant for her to lay with some other man.

Grateful of the wine though wishing that she had taken more, Charity performed what she felt was her duty, terrified that upon any moment Lot would become sober and know her. Yet he seemed not aware. If anything, Charity would have sworn he thought she was Irith. He opened not his eyes. He seemed not to know when she lay down or when she rose at last to leave.

Out in the main area of the cave a while later, Charity stood as in shock. Her garments—gathered and donned immediately upon fleeing that bed—felt hot and heavy as sin.

Ammi was not to be seen.

Not until morning did she encounter her sister. Charity awoke upon her own bed to the sight of Ammi peering in at her from around a stony wall. Her perfect face, long dark hair, as she bit her nails.

Forcing a smile, Charity sat up. "All is well. Come in."

Ammi did gaze upon her sister with wonder in her eyes, a look of anxiety and curiosity. "Did you do as you said you would, then?"

Charity nodded.

"And . . . he did not know it was you?"

"When he was aware at all, he did seem to think I was Mother." Knowing what her sister wished and feared to ask, Charity adjusted her hair and tried comforting her. "It is not what you think. And after a while you forget yourself. I believe the Lord meant it as another expression of love—of course, not as I have done, though I do believe God understands and shall bring blessing out of this uncommon union." She moved a lock of hair away from her sister's eyes. "After all, He did send His angels to save us. Know we not it was *He* who placed us in this situation?"

Like beholding a different person it proved, when in the morning Charity saw their father. Upon asking how he had slept, he replied, "Well enough I suppose, though my head does ache."

Seeing that he had no memory of their union, Charity resolved to continue their plan.

That evening, she plied her father with wine again, suggesting it would mend his aching head. Though reluctant at first, Lot did as bidden. When he went to lay down a little while later, chill wind stirred the women's hair as they looked on each other.

"It is our duty."

"I know, and yet . . . I am afraid," Ammi said, though now her eyes were dry.

Charity reminded her of Enoch's words, as told them by their father, how Cain and Abel must of a certainty have married and lain with their own sisters. "For how else were they to multiply and fill the earth, as the Lord commanded, and as He had known they would need to do? Surely *they* did *their* duty."

She would not force her little sister if she refused, of course.

In the end, Ammi seemed to feel the same compulsion and familial onus. Perhaps *she* also— Charity mused while watching Ammi head toward their father's chamber—felt the same pull of curiosity and push of loneliness. Their father suffered too, and though they meant this not as comfort, they hoped a newborn babe would bring joy in the days ahead alongside a full sense of purpose again.

For all three of them.

In those uncomfortable days which followed, Lot never showed any signs of having known that anyone had come into his chamber and lay down or risen again. Yet never did he take another sip of wine. Neither did he walk before them without full attire, even when spring arrived and with it warm weather.

In those days and in that time both women shown round and full.

Claimed both that they had once lain with their husbands, and Lot questioned them not in this, though Charity had thought he would be angry to find those men had broken their vows to him to lay not a hand upon his daughters until the appointed day.

She chose not to dwell upon such thoughts.

Better to think upon and embrace that oldest of gifts which the Lord had bestowed upon her—that of being great with child.

Chapter Thirteen

When her time came, Charity gave birth to a son, and named him Moab, son of her womb. A later people would declare his name to mean 'Father' (and Charity did wish to honor her father and his), yet also she thought to place a duty upon the boy. It was this second meaning for which she did proclaim the purpose of his name.

Indeed, he would be the *father* of the Moabites.

Not long after this, while Charity suckled her son, Ammi gave birth also to a boychild. She called him Ben-Ammi. He would be the father of the children of Ammon. Even while Ammi lay weary and filled with strange joy, her father (and father of her child), held the boy and smiled.

It did her heart good to see her father rejoice in gladness again.

Truly from that day Lot never again let grief or despair rule over his spirit. Instead he displayed great vigor in caring for these little ones, treating them as his own sons. Helping to raise them in a godly fashion as his own father and his uncle had raised him.

That righteous man who had tortured himself daily in that city of sin, spent his final years in the mountains, raising his sons by his daughters. Training them all up in the way in which they should go.

Teaching them of the Lord's mercy and saving grace.

Singing hymns and spiritual songs.

Providing and giving all he could all the days of his life.

And so when Lot was old and full of days, his daughters laid him to rest in that mount, and as the air was clear and all signs of Sodom and Gomorrah and Zeboiim and Admah had vanished, they and their sons went down from the mountain, just as Noah and his wife and their children had done, so long ago.

For weeks they walked, finding no one, no civilization.

At length however they discovered a city, full of people, brimming with life. Here they settled, not far from where their beloved Uncle (*Father Abram*) had once dwelt with his nephew Lot. After a time however, Charity and Ammi noticed iniquities committed here, sins of a familiar sort they had known elsewhere, and so they departed.

In the course of time, they settled in a country not far from languishing Zoar, and here their sons grew into men. After dispossessing the *Emmi*—a race of large and dangerous men—Moab and Ben-Ammi took wives for themselves and went into them and fathered many sons and daughters of their own.

This testimony did Lot have, because the Lord had found one righteous man in Sodom, and delivered him:

As generations came and went, through the seed of righteous Lot there arose a godly woman named Ruth. Now Ruth, being a Moabitess, in turn met and did marry a godly man of the lineage of

Abraham, named Boaz. Together they begot Obed, who in turn fathered Jesse, the father of King David, the apple of God's eye.

Greatest of earthly kings, it was through the spiritual heritage of good King David that God would provide the King of kings, the Savior for all people.

So God's covenant promise to Abraham through His holy and faithful design, did through His own mysterious unfolding plan, include righteous Lot. Via divers manners did God provide the world His only begotten Son. And though many have questioned Lot's character and offspring, and the manner in which his descendants came about, none can question that the Lord's hand of mercy and grace was ever-present in Lot's days, and throughout his difficult life.

As Enoch had a testimony of righteousness, having walked with God, so too does Lot have this testimony of righteousness, for God has said that a thousand may fall at the right hand and upon the left, but it shall not harm His anointed—and so did He deliver Lot from the destruction of Sodom, where the wicked were judged and punished.

While the righteous were delivered from evil.

Printed in Great Britain
by Amazon

24658091R00108